"Why are you looking at me like that?"

Emily was worried by Lucas's reaction to her dress. It was daring, but that was the point.

"Because the sight of you brings all sorts of things to mind, none of them having anything to do with academic research."

Emily waved a hand at the slip of silk scarlet she was wearing. "But this is all just window dressing. It's not important."

"Do you remember Christmas when you were a kid?"

"Yes." The heat in his eyes made her feel too hot even in her little dress.

"How great the packages all looked wrapped up in shiny paper, and the best part was unwrapping them?"

He looked her over again and his voice dropped an octave. "And the allure of that dress is the fantasy of taking it off...."

"What are the problems and advantages of being beautiful?" That question intrigued **Judith McWilliams** and inspired *Looking Good.* The image of beauty changes with every generation, but society always has expectations of what a woman should be. Judith explores the issue of a woman who seems to have it all—but feels inadequate. A longtime romance fan and writer, Judith makes her home in Indiana.

Books by Judith McWilliams

Looking Good

JUDITH McWILLIAMS

Harlequin Books

TORONTO • NEW YORK • LONDON
AMSTERDAM • PARIS • SYDNEY • HAMBURG
STOCKHOLM • ATHENS • TOKYO • MILAN

Published November 1991

ISBN 0-373-25472-5

LOOKING GOOD

1

"BUT YOU'VE got to help!" Marcy wailed.

"That shows what you know." Emily McGregor continued to sift through the stacks of computer printouts covering her desk.

"But you're the only really beautiful woman I know. It's true," Marcy insisted at her friend's skeptical look. "I mean, look at you. Your hair is so black it has a bluish sheen, your eyes are the color of sapphires, you have a perfect ivory complexion and to cap it all, you've got a figure I'd do anything for except diet. You, my friend, are the epitome of feminine beauty."

And it was all just an illusion, Emily thought with a flash of raw pain. A sham. She fought the pervasive sense of emptiness that had haunted her for the last four months, and forced herself to respond calmly.

"All right, Marcy, I'll concede that I have a combination of physical attributes that our culture has labeled beautiful, but . . ."

"Very good." Marcy nodded approvingly. "You sound exactly like a stuffy college professor. What are you doing? Practicing for your students? The little darlings aren't supposed to arrive on campus till next week."

"Their paperwork precedes them." Emily waved a hand at the computer printouts littering her desk. "I know this is a huge university, but can you believe that all these people are actually taking classes in the history department this fall?"

"So why do you have their paperwork? In the psychology department it all goes to our chairman."

"Ours normally does, too, but Dr. Warren had a family emergency yesterday and had to fly to Los Angeles, so he dumped the whole mess on me."

Marcy's brown eyes brightened speculatively. "I'll bet he's finally going to admit he's beyond it and retire, and he's seeing if you can handle the paperwork before he recommends you for his job."

"Nothing short of a full-blown miracle could handle this!" Emily replied in disgust.

"But it's a great opportunity for you."

"Down, girl." Emily smiled at her friend. "You're only half right. Dr. Warren is finally going to step down as head of the department next year. However, he named me the acting head now, because I'm not in the running for his job."

"What?" Marcy blinked in confusion.

"He said that if he appointed either of the two leading contenders as the acting head, it would be construed as a sign of favoritism. But since I was a woman—excuse me, 'a young woman,'" Emily quoted, "I wouldn't expect to be his ultimate choice, so I wouldn't misunderstand."

"Thirty-two is not young!" Marcy sputtered. "And, if I were you, I'd file a sex-discrimination suit against the twit."

"Tempting, but it would be totally counterproductive. Even if I did win a suit, it would create an intolerable atmosphere to work in. As far as I can see, the best thing to do is what I've always done with sexist remarks—ignore them. Although I almost lost my sense of detachment yesterday and mangled Burt Crisman!"

"If he's the one I think he is, every woman in the university would have lied to provide you with an alibi. What'd the cretin do?"

"You remember that article on Cromwell's domestic policies I wrote for *The History Journal?* Well," Emily continued at Marcy's nod, "I got a letter two days ago asking me to read it at their convention next spring."

"Congratulations!" Marcy beamed at her. "That's quite a feather in your cap. So how's that connected with Crisman?"

"Dr. Warren mentioned it during the departmental meeting and Crisman said that the convention's organizers mustn't have had their quota of female lecturers so they asked me."

"Sour grapes," scoffed Marcy.

"People like him make me so angry!" Emily exclaimed. "As far as they're concerned, if I do something wrong, it's not because I simply made a mistake— it's because I'm a woman. And since women have no business teaching at the college level, of course they're going to make mistakes. But on the other hand, if I do something right, like being asked to present a paper, I don't get the credit. Someone like Crisman will say that I was only asked to make the minority quotas come out right."

"I know exactly what you mean," Marcy responded. "But a good deal of the blame for Crisman has to go to Dr. Warren. That man is a gold-plated, twenty-four-karet male chauvinist. Because of him, jerks like Crisman feel free to express their own warped views."

Emily grimaced. "Don't I know it—although in all fairness, Dr. Warren does have some good points. Remember how supportive he was last spring when . . ."

"So we won't mangle him and stuff his body down the laundry chute," Marcy quipped, trying to distract Emily.

"Stuff his body down a laundry chute?" Emily appreciated her friend's efforts. "Someone ought to censor your reading material."

"Speaking of reading, would you at least look through the specs for the grant? Then you'll see why I need you."

"When? In my copious free time?" Emily asked dryly. "Listen, my friend, the semester is about to start, and in addition to my work, I've got Dr. Warren's, too."

"But you don't have to actually do anything for me until after classes begin," Marcy coaxed.

"Okay. Tell me about your project."

"I'm studying how a woman's physical appearance affects the way people react to her. Almost all of the studies on the subject have dealt with men. And the few that have been aimed at women have been heavy on the philosophical implications and weak on how their findings apply in the real world. I intend to find a way to help women use their physical appearance to project the kind of image they want."

"Hmm." Emily stared at the Snoopy poster on her beige wall as she considered the idea.

"All I need you to do is to help out with the preliminary work. How people react to your appearance will give me an idea of where to concentrate my research. You're perfect because you can easily alter your looks from gorgeous to not so gorgeous. It's much harder to go from plain to beautiful. Take it from one who's tried. At any rate, I'll use graduate students for the actual study. All you two need to do—"

"Two?" Emily was suspicious. "Marcy, this wouldn't be another one of your harebrained schemes to get me dating again, would it?"

"Of course it is," Marcy said sarcastically. "Why, when I received the letter telling me that I'd gotten the grant, my first thought wasn't what a fantastic opportunity this was to do some socially relevant research. Or that the national publicity I'd get when I publish the results would be a terrific boost to my career. No, my first thought was, here's the perfect chance to trick Emily into dating. And then I proceeded to ignore the million-and-one things I had to do before the start of classes and spent the next three days scrutinizing the résumés of every new male faculty member on campus and arranging casual meetings with the most promising candidates so that I could find the man for you."

Emily held up her hand in a fencer's gesture of surrender. "Okay, I apologize. Put like that, I guess it does sound ridiculous."

Marcy wanted to smile with triumph. Her old psychology professor had been right: *The absolute truth delivered in an untruthful manner is never believed.*

"Why include a man if this study is about women?" Emily persisted.

"As a second observer and because some of the tests may require an escort."

"And do you have this sacrificial male lined up?"

"No," Marcy lied, not wanting to spring too much on Emily at once. "Who he is isn't that important," she elaborated on her lie. "All we need is a male body with the right general dimensions."

"Oh?" Emily eyed her friend with fascination. "And which dimensions might those be?"

"Naughty, naughty," Marcy chided. "This is supposed to be serious scientific research."

"Nothing about psychology is scientific," Emily retorted. "Although I will admit that this time you've hit on an intriguing subject."

"Then you'll help?"

"Against my better judgment, I'll help."

"Great! I'll scrounge around and find us a male—"

"With the right dimensions—"

"Who's willing to help," Marcy continued, unperturbed. "I wonder what I can bribe him with?"

"Try promising him that you'll never bother him again."

"Nonsense. Participating in scientific research is a privilege."

"I haven't bought that line since you convinced me to help you with your sleep-deprivation experiment."

"I got an A on it," Marcy reminded smugly.

"Yeah, and I wound up flunking a big history test because I fell asleep in the middle of it."

"I remember. The professor thought you had narcolepsy."

"Instead of just weird friends."

Marcy sighed. "How long ago that seems."

Emily agreed. Then she'd believed she had all the time in the world.

"I should have our man lined up by the reception for new faculty next Thursday night."

"Don't remind me." Emily grimaced. "I loathe that affair."

"So, who doesn't? If you don't hear from me before then, I'll see you there. And good luck with your forms."

Emily watched the door close behind her friend. Marcy simply didn't understand. Emily's operation had been performed months ago, and Marcy believed Emily should get on with her life. Emily agreed with her. Unfortunately, her emotions did not.

It could have been worse, she scolded herself as she returned to her paperwork. She was now completely healthy. She could still have a full, rich life, and she tried hard to believe it.

By the following Thursday evening, Emily had managed to work up some enthusiasm for Marcy's project. It really did sound interesting, and she hoped that Marcy would be able to help women function in today's complex business world. Heaven knew, women could use all the help they could get.

THE MUTED ROAR of hundreds of people talking at the same time became louder as Emily entered the auditorium. "There you are!" Marcy's voice came from behind the scraggly collection of potted plants to the right of the door.

"Why are you hiding?" Emily peered around them to locate her friend. "The whole point of coming to this event is to make sure the president and the chair of your department see you. Then you leave."

"I was waiting for you." Marcy inched out from behind a wilted palm and brushed a dead leaf from the front of her rust-colored dress. "And I must say, you took your own sweet time."

Emily grinned at her. "Must you?"

"At least you look good." Marcy eyed Emily's cobalt-blue silk dress and black high-heeled sandals with approval. "You look very..."

"Professional?" Emily offered.

"Believe me, Mr. Chips never looked like that. Come on. I want to introduce you to our man."

Emily didn't move. "Why?"

"Because it'll make it much easier to work with him if you've been introduced," Marcy replied in a puzzled tone.

"No—I mean why did he agree to help?"

"Because he's new, and this will give him a chance to meet some of the faculty," Marcy explained truthfully, omitting that she'd shown him a picture of Emily.

"Only the stranger part," Emily said ruefully.

"Don't you dare get temperamental on me. This guy is perfect. Not only is he willing, but he was a successful businessman for fifteen years so he'll be able to give us lots of insights about how the corporate world treats women."

"What's he doing here at the university?"

"He sold his computer-software firm last year and accepted a one-year appointment as an executive-in-residence. The business school is ecstatic. Now, come on. I want to introduce you to him before someone corners him."

"I take it he's popular?" Emily obediently followed Marcy as she made her way through the crowd, trying not to breathe too deeply. The mixture of different perfumes and colognes was overpowering.

"Rumor has it that his company sold for over thirty million."

Emily chuckled. "That's popularity on a grand scale."

"You'd better believe it," Marcy said in disgust. "Greed is a great motivator. Ah, there he is."

"Where?" Emily peered around the oversize woman in front of her, searching for someone who looked like a high-powered businessman.

"There—" Marcy pointed "—to the right of Dr. Welbourne. Wait here. I'll go get him."

Emily turned slightly to get a good look at the man Dr. Welbourne was talking to so earnestly.

His six-foot frame was dressed in a gray suit that had obviously been custom tailored. The gleaming white of his shirt contrasted with his deep tan. His head was tilted to one side as he listened, throwing the sharply chiseled planes of his face into stark relief.

Emily focused on his firm lips. As if drawn by the intensity of her stare, the man looked at her. A sudden gleam flared to life in his hazel eyes and a slow, sensual smile curved his mouth, sending warmth through her body.

Emily blinked under the impact of her unexpected reaction to him. He should be wearing a sign with Danger printed on it in big red letters.

She watched as Marcy detached him from Dr. Welbourne and led him to her.

"Emily, I'd like you to meet Lucas Sheridan. Lucas, this is Emily McGregor."

Automatically, Emily held out her hand, barely repressing a shudder when Lucas's calloused fingers closed around it. Rippling waves of sensation poured over her skin, flooding her nerve endings and sending a hectic flush along her cheeks.

"It's a pleasure to meet you, Dr. McGregor." The conventionality of his words released her from the strange spell he'd cast over her.

"Oh, for goodness' sake, call her Emily. Then she can call you Lucas," Marcy said with a heartiness that Emily thoroughly mistrusted.

"Emily?" She gave him a noncommittal smile. Insisting that he address her by her title would make him wonder why she was being so formal, and she didn't want him curious about her. She didn't want *any* man curious about her.

"Marcy was explaining to me what she hoped to accomplish with her research," he said, "and it sounds—"

"Lucas, my boy!" Dean Goodman of the School of Business slapped Lucas on the shoulder. "I've been looking all over for you. There's a visiting professor from Austria I want you to meet. I left him over by the punch bowl. You don't mind, do you, ladies?"

"Of course not," Emily agreed, before Marcy could object. "That's what this reception is for—getting to know people."

"An interesting concept," Lucas murmured with a wicked gleam in his eyes.

Emily kept her expression carefully blank as if she hadn't caught the innuendo.

"I'll stop by your office later in the week and we can discuss the project, Emily," Lucas called over his shoulder as he left with the dean.

"But—" Emily found herself talking to the empty air. Damn! She most definitely didn't want Lucas in her office. If he affected her this strongly in public, how would she respond to him in private?

"Well, what do you think?" Marcy demanded. "Can I pick them or what?"

"*What* being the operative word. Such as, what would make a man like that agree to help us?"

"I told you. To get to know people. He's a stranger in Wilmington. In fact, this is the first time he's ever been in Indiana."

"At the rate Dean Goodman is introducing him, he'll know everyone by tomorrow."

"Lucas said he'd help, and he strikes me as a man of his word," Marcy insisted.

"Among other things."

"You don't like him?"

"What's not to like?" Emily questioned in return. Marcy was much too astute not to see an emphatic rejection of Lucas for exactly what it was—fear. Fear of getting involved and, ultimately, rejected.

But maybe Lucas could be maneuvered into backing out himself. If she were to be too busy to meet with him every time he called, he might decide that helping Marcy was too much trouble. Especially after the amount of attention he was getting tonight. Unless she missed her guess, he was going to be inundated with invitations. What was it Jane Austen had said—that society assumed a bachelor in possession of a fortune automatically stood in need of a wife?

Emily wasted no time in putting her plan into action. Each time Lucas called to discuss their project, she pleaded busyness and sidestepped his attempts to pin her down to a meeting. She salved her guilty conscience by telling herself that Lucas wasn't really necessary to Marcy's study. *Any* man would do.

FOUR DAYS AFTER the reception, there was a brisk knock at Emily's open office door. She looked up from the class lists to see Lucas filling the doorway. He shouldn't have, she thought distractedly. He wasn't much more than four inches taller than she was, but somehow his personality exuded a vibrancy that expanded to fill the available space. A vibrancy that Emily could feel lifting the fine hairs on her arms. Lucas Sheridan's effect on her had not been a one-time fluke.

"Have I caught you at a bad time?" He stepped into the tiny room and searched for a chair. There wasn't one.

"Sorry, I hid the chair in the storage room at the end of the hall."

"No problem. I'll just sit here." He pushed aside a stack of computer printouts on the edge of her desk and sat down. The fine brown wool of his suit pants stretched across the hard muscles of his thighs.

Using the need to file her papers as an excuse, Emily escaped to the oak cabinet in the corner. Lucas frowned at her obvious retreat.

So he hadn't been imagining things, he realized. Emily McGregor was trying to brush him off. She'd been extremely wary of him at the president's reception; her voice had been cool and distancing every time he'd called, and now that he'd forced the issue, she was practically running away from him.

He studied the rigid line of her back as she bent over the filing cabinet. She looked tense enough to break. But why? He had done nothing more than show normal appreciation for a beautiful woman. And with her looks, she had to be used to men finding her attractive.

So, why was she withdrawing? It was almost as if she was afraid of him. But he'd done nothing to threaten her and, since Marcy approved of him, she wouldn't have prejudiced Emily against him. On the surface, her reaction simply didn't make sense.

Unless . . . Was she coming out of a bad experience with a man? Could her negative reaction be to him as a member of the male sex and not to him as a distinct personality?

If he wanted to get to know Emily—and he most emphatically did—he was going to have to get past her defenses. But how? Emily was a teacher and, from what Marcy had said, a very good one. He suddenly realized she would be most comfortable in a teacher-student kind of relationship. It would give her the illusion of being in charge. But what could he ask her to teach him? He'd think about it later, he decided. At the moment, it was more important to keep the conversation impersonal and nonthreatening.

"Do you always hide your chairs or was it just on my behalf?" he asked.

"I didn't know you were coming." Her tone of voice left Lucas in no doubt that if she had, she wouldn't have been there. "I always get rid of it at the beginning of the term to cut down on the whining and complaints."

"That sounds like quite a chair. Have you considered taking it over to the theology department and letting them have a go at exorcising its evil spirts?"

Emily laughed, relaxing at his teasing banter. "Not the chair's whining, the students'. It took me a couple of years to figure out that if they aren't comfortable, they don't complain half as long."

"Do they complain a lot? I taught my first class this morning, and I was very favorably impressed by the general maturity of my students."

"Let me guess. Graduate level?"

"Uh-huh. Business ethics."

"My graduate students are great, too, but I'm also adviser to twenty-five freshmen, and some of them find college a little overwhelming at first."

"I—" He broke off as someone beat urgently on the door.

"Come in," Emily called.

The door swung open, and a harried-looking young man burst in. "I want out."

"But you just got here," Lucas murmured under his breath.

Emily gave Lucas a quelling glance and turned back to the young man. "Perhaps if you were to give me your name and explain the nature of your problem?"

"Ryan Jones and I told you. I want out. I don't want to take Russian. It was awful!" He shuddered. "I sat through the whole class, and I didn't understand a word. Not a word!"

"Don't worry," Emily said soothingly. Trying to ignore Lucas's presence, she sat at her desk and reached for the keyboard of her computer. The movement brought her close enough to Lucas to smell the faintly spicy aroma of his cologne. Gamely, she ignored her unsettling reaction and asked Ryan for his social security number and keyed it in. "You're a freshman with an undecided major?"

"Yeah, but I sure know what it isn't going to be."

"And your Beginning Russian class was held in Landis Hall, Room 114?"

"Yeah, and it took forever to find," he complained. "I tried to take a shortcut and got lost."

"Hmm." Emily frowned. "You say there was no English spoken at all?"

"None. The only thing English was the instructor's name written on the board."

"What was it?"

"Blandings."

Emily checked the campus directory, then picked up her phone and dialed the number listed.

"Dr. Blandings, this is Emily McGregor in the history department. One of the freshmen I advise has just returned from— Yes, that's right. Red hair, blue eyes and wearing jeans. I see." Her lips tightened in annoyance as she listened to Blandings.

"And it didn't occur to you to tell him? . . . Perhaps, but what he's more likely to remember is your deliberate lack of kindness." She hung up the phone with a snap and turned to the young man.

"You weren't in a Beginning Russian class. You were in a senior-level literature class on Tolstoy."

"But . . . I was in the right room. I know I was. I double-checked before I disturbed them."

"It seems that the beginning class was larger than anticipated and the literature class smaller, so the professors switched rooms. Your class is now in Landis 318."

"But why didn't he tell me?" Ryan asked.

"He announced it before class started. You arrived late. He says that if you want to know things, you have to get there on time," said Emily, repeating the professor's words.

"That sucks!"

"So does your choice of vocabulary," Lucas interjected.

A deep red flush stained Ryan's cheeks, highlighting his youth. "Sorry, sir. Sorry, Dr. McGregor."

"S'okay." Emily gave him a sympathetic smile. "Just hang in there, and don't let the turkeys get you down. After a week or so, things will seem a lot easier."

"If you say so," Ryan replied doubtfully.

"Poor kid," Lucas said once he'd left. "What's with this Blandings character?"

"Nothing that isn't wrong with a great many other professors. They regard the students as a necessary evil to be endured so that they can do what they really want—research."

Lucas frowned.

"If you left the business world looking for Utopia, this isn't it," she said seriously.

"Utopia isn't a place, Emily. It's a state of mind usually induced by a very special person."

Emily stared at him as the thought of what it would be like to be that special person for Lucas Sheridan filled her mind. To be the focus of his thoughts and needs. It might, indeed, be Utopia. But not for her, she reminded herself. Never for her. Not with Lucas Sheridan or any other man. She was flawed.

"Emily?" Lucas reached for her only to draw back as the door burst open and a young woman rushed in.

"Dr. McGregor!"

"Is the building on fire?" Lucas inquired.

The girl's eyes widened as she took a good look at him, and she gave him a beaming smile that annoyed Emily.

"No, why?" the girl asked.

"The fact that you didn't bother to knock made me think it was an emergency."

"It is." The girl remembered her grievance and turned to Emily. "Dr. McGregor, you've just got to switch me to another instructor. The one I've got is a fiend!"

"And I'm totally in the dark," Emily said patiently. "Who are you, what class are we talking about and who's a fiend?"

"I'm Jessie Bricklin. It's History of Western Civilization I, and Dr. Spalding is the fiend."

"Wait a minute. Are we talking about the same Dr. Spalding? About five-two, late sixties, white hair, black eyes?"

"Yeah, I guess he did look like that," Jessie admitted. "But it doesn't matter what he looks like. It's what he said."

"If Dr. McGregor isn't interested in what he said, I am," Lucas finally inserted when Emily simply stared at the girl.

"He said we had to read three outside books, do a midterm paper at least ten pages long and that all our tests would be essays." Her voice rose to an indignant shriek. "You've got to get me out of his class!"

"There's a second alternative," Lucas suggested. "I almost hesitate to say it, but you could try studying."

"But—" Jessie began.

"No," Emily said flatly. "I refuse to listen to one more word. You listen to me, for a change. Freshmen rarely get a chance to take a class with a professor of Dr.

Spalding's standing. The only reason you are is because he's a passionate advocate of undergraduate education—even for those students who don't have the sense to realize what they're being offered."

"But—"

"I will not authorize your transfer simply because you think it might involve some work."

"But I won't have time to do anything else!" Jessie wailed.

"There's a lecture tonight at the Student Union on how to organize your time," Emily continued unsympathetically. "I suggest you attend."

"Just you wait!" Jessie challenged. "I'm going to call my father, and he'll call the president of this stupid school and then you'll be sorry!" She stormed out of the office, slamming the door behind her.

Emily winced as the glass in her one window rattled. "Putting that girl in a class with a historian of Dr. Spalding's caliber has to be what's meant by casting pearls before swine."

"I'm beginning to be grateful that I'm only teaching graduate students," Lucas remarked.

"Well, in all fairness, the vast majority of freshmen aren't anywhere near that bad, and even Jessie will probably shape up and get to work once she realizes that Daddy isn't going to be able to intimidate President Pulkowski."

"Speaking of working, have you given any thought to exactly what it is we're going to do for Marcy's project?"

"A little. Marcy wants us to try out a variety of situations that the average woman might find herself in. This should give her some ideas on where to concentrate the actual study." Emily ran her fingers through her shoulder-length curls and leaned back in her chair, trying to make her withdrawal appear natural. She found it difficult to think clearly with Lucas so close, but her pride demanded that she not let him realize it.

"That sounds logical. Start with the general and narrow your possibilities to the specific," he said thoughtfully. "How long do we have to do our research?"

"Well, Marcy wants to start the actual study around the middle of October, and she'll need a few weeks to analyze our data. So, we should finish our test by the end of September."

"That only gives us a month. We'll need to begin as soon as possible."

"Have you ever done any academic research?" Emily questioned.

"No, but I've commissioned market research for my company in the past, and the principles ought to be the same."

"Perhaps we've—" A thump on the door stopped her.

"Is it always like this?" Lucas asked in exasperation.

"Just a minute," she called. "This is just the first day of classes. Things will have calmed down by next week."

"What time do you finish here?"

"I told my students that I'd be available until six tonight."

"Then, how about if we make our plans over dinner?"

"Dinner?" She stalled, knowing that Lucas Sheridan represented a very real threat to her hard-won calm. Her uncharacteristic reaction to him was ample proof of that. Meeting him in a social circumstance could only make the situation worse. With uncharacteristic indecision, she bit her lower lip.

"By six I'm going to be too tired to go out," she finally answered.

"I can certainly understand that." He gave her a sympathetic smile that made her feel cherished. "Tell you what—how about if I cook dinner tonight?"

"Thank you," Emily said, realizing that a refusal would give rise to exactly the kind of speculation she wanted to avoid.

"I live in the Markham apartments over on Ohio Street. I'll expect you shortly after six. And good luck this afternoon. It appears you're going to need it."

Not as much as I'm going to need it this evening, she reflected.

2

EMILY HAD NEVER BEEN in the Markham Towers before. Not only was it a relatively new building, but its high rent made it too expensive for most of the people she knew. She eyed the uniformed guard behind the mahogany reception desk, wondering if there really was a need for security in a sleepy little college town of barely forty thousand people.

"Yes, miss?" The guard studied the way Emily's tan linen slacks clung to her long legs, and his polite smile warmed perceptibly. "May I help you?"

"I'm here to see Lucas Sheridan."

"Ah, yes. Mr. Sheridan left word that you'd be arriving. The elevator's there." He pointed to his left. "His apartment is on the top floor, number C."

Emily stepped into the open elevator, vaguely unnerved by the excitement she felt at seeing Lucas again. *This is work,* she reminded herself. *He's simply a colleague with whom you're doing research.*

The problem was, Lucas didn't treat her like a colleague. He quite obviously didn't have the vaguest idea about proper protocol between two academics involved in research. He was much too friendly, clearly seeing her as a woman first and a colleague second—although he had been neither obvious nor offensive about it. Nor, on the other hand, had he shown any inclination to discount her mind simply because he found the body that housed it attractive.

Perhaps she should give him a few hints on the way to treat his fellow professors? But not right away. She would tell him once they'd finished and he was feeling a little more at ease in a university environment. Launching a teaching career was more than enough for him to cope with right now.

The elevator doors opened with a subdued chime, and Emily stepped out into the wide hallway of the fifth floor. Apartment C was at the end of the corridor, and Emily took a deep breath to counter her sudden feeling of anticipation. If only. . . Resolutely, she refused to allow the thought to form; dwelling on might-have-beens was unproductive.

Emily glanced down to make sure her orange silk blouse was still tucked in, brushed the shoulders of her cream linen blazer, and rang the doorbell.

No one answered. Emily waited, trying to decide whether ringing again would make her seem over-eager, when the door was suddenly flung open.

"Hurry up." Lucas grabbed her arm and yanked her into the apartment. "I've reached the critical stage."

"In your sanity hearing, no doubt," she replied, eyeing him dubiously. His dark brown hair was disheveled as if he'd been running his fingers through it; the front of his pale blue knit shirt was covered with tiny red splotches; and the worn jeans that so attractively molded his flat abdomen and muscular thighs were also covered by a light dusting of what appeared to be flour.

"I'm cooking your dinner. I—" There was a sudden hiss followed by a loud popping sound, and Lucas tensed.

"Excuse me." He raced to the small kitchen.

More cautiously, Emily followed him. She found him peering helplessly into a large frying pan that was spraying an oily liquid onto the copper-tone stovetop. She wrinkled her nose at the acrid smell.

"I'm browning the butter," he announced, glancing to see how she was reacting to his carefully contrived disaster. It wasn't until he'd started to assemble the ingredients for the meal that the idea had come to him. He'd ask her to teach him to cook. It was perfect. Society still often portrayed bachelors as bumbling idiots in the kitchen, so she'd be predisposed to believe that he didn't have a clue. And, best of all, it was something they could do together. Close together.

Emily looked again at the pan on the stove. "Wrong. You're *burning* the butter. You'd better take it off the heat."

"Yes." He grabbed the skillet's handle. With a startled yelp, he immediately let go and began to blow on his reddened fingers.

"It's hot!" He glared accusingly at the pan.

"Probably a result of sitting on an electric coil turned on too high." Emily stifled a giggle at his aggrieved expression.

He ignored her as he looked around the small kitchen. "Where's that damn pot holder?"

"Spirited away by gremlins, no doubt." She studied the kitchen with disbelief.

Pans, dripping bowls, various cooking utensils and ingredients littered every inch of the kitchen's limited counter space. A large red stain smeared the cream-colored linoleum floor next to what looked like a pool of beaten egg. A wet dishcloth had been carelessly tossed over the edge of the sink and was slowly dripping water onto the floor. How could things be this messy when he'd just moved in?

Another angry hiss from the scorching butter seemed to goad Lucas into action. He grabbed a dish towel from the counter, wrapped it around the handle and pushed the skillet onto the cold back burner. In the process, the towel's fringe brushed across the glowing red coil and instantly burst into flames.

Lucas dropped the towel on the stovetop and, grabbing a metal spatula, tried to beat the flames out. Unfortunately, his vigorous thumping only served to tear the blazing cloth into smaller, still-burning pieces. Lucas tossed the spatula aside and picked up a roll of paper towels. Using it as a club, he began to pound the flaming remnants of material.

"I don't think that's a good idea." Emily's warning came a second too late. The roll of towels ignited.

"Damnation!" Lucas flung the roll into the sink and turned on the water faucet. Using the bottom of the brass teakettle, he finally managed to smother the burning bits of towel.

"There." He gave her a victorious smile as he replaced the now soot-stained kettle on the stove. "It's just a matter of—"

An expression of genuine horror crossed his face as the piercing wail of the kitchen's smoke alarm filled the small room. "Damn! Damn! Damn!" Grabbing the large packing box sitting under the breakfast bar, he shoved it into position beneath the screaming alarm. Climbing into the box, he reached up to disconnect the alarm. The box lid sagged under his weight, and he momentarily lost his balance.

Emily grabbed for him, closing her arms around his knees as she steadied him against her shoulder. The soft denim of his jeans brushed against her face for a second before the hard muscles of his thigh pressed into her cheek.

"There." The satisfied tone of his voice shook Emily out of her abstraction, and she hastily stepped back. To her relief, Lucas didn't seem to have noticed her inattention. He had managed to pry open the plastic cover of the alarm and was in the process of removing the battery. Finally, it yielded to his tugs and the noise abruptly ceased. He jumped down and pushed the box out of the way.

"I've read comics where people had the fire department standing by when they cook, but I didn't realize that they actually existed," she said tartly.

He looked around the kitchen in a dazed manner as if overwhelmed by the whole fiasco. "I'm not quite sure what happened. I even bought a cookbook that came with pictures."

"It should have come with a fire extinguisher. What did I almost get for dinner?"

"Steak Eszterhazy."

Emily blinked. "Steak what?"

"It's top-round steak served with a rich, piquant sauce and garnished with strips of parsnips, carrots and gherkins," he quoted the cookbook.

"Rather ambitious. How much actual cooking experience have you had?"

"Cooking is simply a matter of common sense," he hedged.

"None." Emily drew her own conclusion. "If I were you, I'd take that book back to wherever it was you got it and exchange it for a basic how-to manual."

"I can't. It was the first casualty when the tomato exploded. How about if I run out and get a pizza while you start cleaning up?" He gestured around the kitchen, exercising an iron control to keep his excitement from showing. Emily was falling for his plan.

Emily barely suppressed a shudder. "How about if I go for pizza and you clean up?"

"But—"

"After all, it's your kitchen and your mess."

"But I was trying to cook your dinner."

"Hasn't anyone ever told you that the road to hell is paved with good intentions?"

"Hell is right!" Lucas eyed the still-smoldering roll of paper towels in the sink. "All right, you go get the pizza and leave me alone with the disaster."

"Of your own making." Emily refused to sympathize. There was no way she was going to allow herself to be conned into doing his dirty work. Not after the day she'd just put in. "What do you want on your pizza?"

"Everything, and get a big one. I'm starved." The bright gleam in his eyes invested his seemingly innocent words with all kinds of hidden meanings—meanings Emily didn't feel up to coping with at the moment, so she ignored them. "Fine. I'll be back in half an hour."

Her estimate turned out to be overly optimistic. A large part of the student body had decided to celebrate the first day of classes with pizza, and she had to wait in line. It was over an hour later before she returned with the pizza and a cold six-pack of soda.

She had barely touched the bell of his apartment when the door was flung open.

"There you are," he said, with obvious relief at the sight of her. "I was beginning to think you weren't coming back."

Emily handed him the drinks, wondering if it was her he was so eager to see or his dinner.

"No beer?"

"The pizza parlor doesn't have a liquor license, and I don't like beer well enough to make a second stop." She looked around the living room for a table, frowning when she realized there wasn't one. In fact, other than moving boxes, there wasn't any furniture of any sort.

"What's the matter?" Lucas asked, in a carefully casual voice. Since he'd moved in on Wednesday, he'd been sleeping on an old camp cot. His original plan had been to buy some furniture this weekend—a plan he'd amended after watching Emily interact with her students. Beneath her highly competent exterior lurked a very kind heart, which he hoped would lead her to offer to help him pick out some furniture. It was certainly worth trying. Anything that threw them together was worth trying.

"Where's your dining-room table? Or something to sit on, for that matter?"

"I haven't got one. I've been sitting on the floor."

He pulled over one of the packing boxes, set the pizza on it and sat down on the carpet. "Have a seat. It's great for your spine."

"You wouldn't happen to be some kind of physical-fitness nut, would you?" She eyed him suspiciously.

"No. Just busy. I liked this building, but it didn't have any furnished units. So I took an unfurnished apartment, planning to buy my own furniture."

"So, why haven't you bought any yet? Or are all the stories circulating about your money just fairy tales?"

"What tales?"

"That you made millions when you sold your company. Lots of millions."

"Is that why Marcy asked me to help her in her research?" he questioned slowly. "Because she thought I was wealthy and could fund it?"

"No, she doesn't need any financial help. She really does have a government grant. She undoubtedly picked on you because you're new."

"Why is that an advantage?"

Emily chuckled. "Because anyone who's been around the university for any length of time knows better than to get mixed up in the psychology department's research projects. Marcy has to grab her victims while they're still naive."

"Naive?" he repeated.

Emily watched in fascination as his lips slowly lifted in a sensual smile.

No. Lucas Sheridan might be many things, but he wasn't naive. And probably hadn't been since grade school. He was watching her with an intent look. She blinked and the expression vanished, leaving her to wonder if she'd simply imagined the whole thing. He was turning out to be a surprisingly complicated man, as well as an oddly appealing one. Even if she had no intention of getting involved with him on a man-woman basis, surely there could be no harm if they were friends.

She watched as he ate his way through a piece of pizza with the single-minded concentration of the starving. "So, tell me about your furniture or the lack thereof," she said, steering the conversation onto neutral ground.

"I was intimidated."

"Sure you were," she scoffed.

"No, it's true," he insisted, playing the poor-male-out-of-his-depth for all he was worth. "As soon as the movers unloaded last week, I went to that big furniture store over by the mall."

"So what happened?" Emily prodded when he scowled at the memory.

"I had a list. I was going to get a bed and a dresser, a table and a sofa and chairs for the living room. And then the questions started."

"Questions? Like what?"

"Like what was my color scheme? What period did I want? Did I want a down sofa or a foam one? Hideaway or steel-framed?" He grimaced. "I wanted something to sit on, and they wanted to analyze my life-style. So I left."

Emily shifted on the hard floor. "I guess you showed them."

"I'm going to have to try again," he conceded. "I'm not as young as I used to be."

"Few of us are." A feeling of bleakness invaded her as she remembered just how old she'd felt ever since . . .

"But you aren't sleeping on a camp cot," his voice broke in. "I've got aches in muscles I didn't even know I had."

"Oh?" Emily's gaze wandered over his broad chest, lingering on his prominent biceps.

"You know," he began slowly, hoping his timing was right. "You could help."

Emily's breath caught in her throat at the thought of helping his aching muscles, of putting her hands on his bare skin and kneading—

"Being a historian and all, you'd probably know what she was talking about."

Emily blinked and the delightful image vanished. She scrambled to follow his line of thought rather than hers.

"How so?" she probed for a clue.

"Periods of furniture. That kind of thing."

"But I'm not the one who'll have to live with it."

He snorted. "You sound just like that salesperson in the furniture store. One doesn't live with a sofa. One sits on it."

"You, sir, are a Philistine. And a hungry one at that."

He reached for another piece of pizza. "I'm a realist."

Emily frowned at the unexpected hint of steel in his voice, wondering if she was being warned.

"A desperate realist." He softened his tone. "Would you come along with me tomorrow and help me?"

"I can't." Emily ignored her instinctive impulse to agree. "Tomorrow's the one Saturday that the local orchard lets the public pick their own apples. I always get a bushel to make my year's supply of applesauce."

"Make?"

"You know—can, preserve."

"Why would you do that when any grocery store has shelves full of applesauce?"

"Sure, and who knows what the manufacturers put in it when the FDA isn't looking."

"Saltpeter?" he suggested.

"What?"

"Saltpeter. I saw a movie once where they kept all the men in the army from straying into town by adding saltpeter to their oatmeal. They—"

"Never mind." Emily was feeling unsettled enough. She most emphatically didn't need a discussion on men's sexual urges or their suppression. "The point I was trying to make is that it takes time to pick out furniture, and I have to make my applesauce," she insisted.

"Tell you what, if you help me, I'll help you smash your apples." Then he sprung the trap: "It must be nice to be able to cook."

Emily looked up and was lost at his wistful expression. An unexpected surge of tenderness engulfed her. Lucas looked so helpless. And even though she suspected that he was about as helpless as a Sherman tank, she was unable to resist the appeal. "I suppose I could teach you the rudiments of cooking."

He beamed at her, relief washing over him. She'd bought his act. "My stomach thanks you. Now, all that's left is my poor aching bones . . . ."

Emily laughed. "You forgot to mention your persistence. Very well. I'll hold your hand while you brave the furniture store. If we go as soon as the store opens, we'll still have plenty of time to do the apples."

"Do you want those little bits of pepperoni left on the bottom of the box?" He looked longingly at them.

"No. What I want is to discuss how we're going to set up our research. We need to get started next week."

"Yes, careful planning is essential to the realization of any goal," he said.

Emily frowned, experiencing the strange feeling that they were talking about two different things.

"I thought we could start small," she finally said when he didn't elaborate.

"How small?" Lucas finished the pepperoni and started on the mushroom pieces.

"I could try returning a sale item to Winthrops. The local department store," she explained at his blank look. "It's not allowed."

He frowned in confusion. "The local department store?"

"No, returning sale items. I'll try it first as myself and then as a less attractive version of myself." Emily stared off into space. "I think I'll have a talk with Catherine Parr."

"Catherine Parr? The name sounds vaguely familiar. Did I meet her last night?"

"Possibly. She's in the theater department. But what's more likely is that her name sounds familiar because Catherine Parr was one of Henry VIII's wives."

"If she was one of Henry VIII's wives, she should be in the parapsychology department."

"You'd better not try any bad jokes about her name on her," Emily warned him. "After listening to them for thirty-odd years, she tends to be a little intolerant."

"Sorry." The twinkle in his eye belied his apology. "I had an idea for the study. An old friend of mine who lives here in town owns a plastic company. He has a receptionist who greets everyone who comes into the factory's offices and directs them to where they want to go. Why don't I see if he'll let you sub for her one day?"

"Great!" Emily said enthusiastically. "That way we could test lots of people's reactions in a short period of time. Do you think he'll agree?"

"I don't see why not. I'll give him a ring over the weekend and ask."

"I could also try getting a seat on a crowded bus, and a table in a restaurant one Saturday evening without a reservation," she continued.

"How busy can a restaurant in a town this size be?"

"On a home football weekend? You wouldn't believe the number of people who descend on the university to watch a bunch of kids fling a pigskin around a muddy field."

"Having seen the team's losing percentage, I probably wouldn't."

"You don't like football?" Emily eyed him with sudden interest.

"I've never been a fan of failure, whether it's organized or not. Now, Notre Dame's football . . ." His eyes took on a fanatical gleam that Emily had no trouble interpreting. It was a look that was rampant on campus during basketball season.

She sighed. "Never mind. I knew it was too good to be true. At any rate, we can add visiting a restaurant during a home game to our list." She got to her feet. "I also want to try letting people approach me."

Picking up the empty pizza box, she went to the kitchen to dispose of it. "Where's your wastebasket?" she asked when she couldn't find it.

"I don't have one. Just dump the box on the counter."

Emily grimaced as she set it down beside a stack of dirty bowls. Offering to teach Lucas to cook might not have been one of her better ideas.

"What did you normally eat for dinner before you moved here?"

"Restaurant food. I tended to work fifteen-hour days. So I'd just have something sent in."

"It's a wonder you haven't dropped dead from a heart attack."

"I'm healthy as a horse," he countered. "I exercise forty-five minutes every other day on a ski machine. It's a great workout."

"That is a contradiction in terms. If God had meant us to exercise, we'd have been born wearing sneakers."

"Or brains," he said. "You said you want to let people approach you. How do you intend to do it?"

"I thought I'd sit at a bar and see what happens. You can sit at the other end and keep an eye on things," she added when he frowned.

"I don't like it. Bars are . . ." He gestured impotently.

"Basic meeting places," she filled in. "Don't be stuffy."

"Stuffy!" His eyes glittered with annoyance. "I am not stuffy. I simply don't like bars. Not only do they tend to be full of chauvinistic men—"

"You mean there's another kind?" Emily gave him a look of wide-eyed wonder.

He grimaced. "Very funny. I still don't like it."

"How about if I check with Marcy and see what she thinks?"

"I guess," he conceded grudgingly.

"Now then—" she steeled herself to make the effort "—just to show you that my heart's in the right place, I'll help you clean up."

Lucas's gaze slowly shifted to her chest and Emily felt her skin heat under his scrutiny. It wasn't a feeling she welcomed. She didn't want Lucas to flirt with her; she wanted him to be her friend, with no sexual overtones—although that might be asking the impossible, she acknowledged. Lucas Sheridan was a very appealing man, and she had the sneaking suspicion that beneath the civilized exterior, was a strong core of primitive male. The thought filled her with a confusing mixture of nervousness and excitement.

"Don't worry about the kitchen," he told her. "I'll clean up later. Why don't you go home and get a good night's sleep. You're going to have a busy day tomorrow."

She was? Emily blinked at the tiny reflections gleaming in his eyes and her stomach contracted in a combination of wariness and curiosity. What had she let herself in for?

3

THE INSISTENT BUZZ of the doorbell beat against Emily's reluctant consciousness. She groaned a protest and rolled over, pulling the thick down pillow over her head. It helped slightly, but not enough to entirely deaden the sound. It continued with the persistence of a swarm of bees.

In disgust, Emily flung the pillow to the foot of the bed. She forced open her eyelids and peered blearily at the bedside clock. Its glowing red numbers mocked her.

"Six-thirty? Six-thirty!" Furious, she marched to her front door, intent on first silencing the bell and then demolishing whatever sadist had been misguided enough to drag her out of bed at six-thirty on a Saturday morning.

Emily flung open the door and snapped, "Stop that infernal racket!"

"Testy this morning, aren't we?" Marcy's cheerful voice responded.

"Testy enough to commit murder. What are you doing here at this unearthly hour?"

"I've been up for ages, and I've run three miles," Marcy said virtuously, "while you've been sleeping your life away."

"Sleeping...!" Emily exclaimed. "In the first place, it's Saturday and in the second, I didn't get to bed till almost two."

"Oh?" Marcy questioned. "Invite me in for coffee, and you can tell Aunt Marcy all about your late night."

"You already are in." Emily closed the door with a sigh. "And there's nothing to tell. I was up reading the proposal for one of my doctoral students' dissertations."

Emily pushed her tumbled hair out of her face, stretched and then staggered to the kitchen. Actually, coffee wasn't such a bad idea. A hefty dose of caffeine could only help her sluggish mental processes.

Marcy perched on a stool at the breakfast bar and announced, "You know, Emily, it's a good thing I like you, because otherwise I'd hate you."

Emily carefully measured coffee into the pot, flipped on the coffeemaker and then said, "That should be my line. I'm the one who got rousted out of bed for no good reason."

Marcy ignored the comment, preferring to follow her own line of thought. "I mean, look at you. You're only half awake. You're wearing a disreputable robe that by all rights should make you look like an oversize rabbit, you have no makeup on, and your hair is falling every which way. And do you know what you look like?"

"If it's anything like I feel, then hell."

"You look gorgeous. Absolutely gorgeous. There's simply no justice in the world."

"Oh, yes, there is." Emily's voice was bitter. "It all evens out in the end. You may not have my looks, but you can have children."

"That's true," Marcy admitted. "But, Emily, you've never shown the slightest desire to have a child before. Or even to get married."

"But I was going to." Emily struggled to make her understand. "At some point in the future I fully intended to marry and have a child. Exactly when was my choice to make, but now the choice isn't mine anymore. My hysterectomy has made me less of a woman."

"That's ridiculous!" Marcy sputtered. "You're every bit as much a woman as you ever were."

Emily looked sadly at her friend. "Women may have come a long way, but society still measures a woman's basic worth by her ability to have children. It's true," she insisted when Marcy frowned. "Think about all the articles you read in magazines about when is the best time for a woman to have children so as to cause the least disruption in her career. Our society may have opened up all kinds of job opportunities for women, but they're in addition to our primary role as mothers, not instead of."

"But even if some of what you say is true, and I'm not admitting it is, there are still lots of couples who don't have children," Marcy argued. "They seem to have happy, fulfilling relationships."

"If the decision not to have children is a mutual one, it can work out," Emily conceded. "Or even if two people fell in love before they found out that one of them is sterile, then they at least have their love to fall back on. But don't you see, Marcy? It's different with me."

"No, I don't see."

"Then you're being willfully blind," Emily said tiredly. "I already know that I can't have children. I can't marry and then tell my husband the truth after the wedding."

"So, tell him before."

"*When* before? At what point in the relationship do I casually toss into the conversation, 'Oh, by the way, have I mentioned lately that I've had a hysterectomy?' I can hardly tell a man something that personal when we first start dating because it implies that I've got him lined up as a prospective husband. And I guarantee you that nothing is deadlier to a developing relationship than to suggest that you have permanency in mind."

"You could wait until you got to know him a little better."

"How much better? Until I'm sure that I want a future with him? Until I'm in love with him? What if his response is, 'I'm really sorry, but kids are important to me'? Then I'm left nursing a broken heart. Or, even worse, what if he really wanted kids, but said it didn't matter because he pitied me? That would be a great basis for a marriage."

Emily filled a mug with the freshly brewed coffee and handed it to Marcy, then poured one for herself. She leaned against the counter and peered at the silent Marcy. "Don't tell me I've finally managed to shut you up."

Marcy grimaced. "I guess you've got a point. I hadn't really considered the logistics of exactly how one tells a man something like that. It could be tricky, but there has to be a way."

"Do tell. I'm all ears."

"You sound all mouth."

"What did you expect, getting me out of bed at this ungodly hour?" Emily took a reviving sip of coffee. "Although now that you're here, tell me what you think about bars."

"Bars?" Marcy blinked and looked down at the breakfast bar in front of her.

"Not that kind of bar. The kind that serves liquor."

"In what context?"

"Well, Lucas and I were making some specific plans for your study last night and—"

"Last night?" Marcy pounced. "I thought he said he was going to see you in your office."

"He did. He also saw a number of disgruntled students there. One who had very good reason to be upset." Emily frowned in remembrance. "At any rate, we couldn't get anything done, so he invited me over to his place."

"To see his etchings?" Marcy raised her eyebrows.

"If he has any, they're still packed away. He just moved in. In fact, I'm helping him to pick out furniture this morning."

"You lucky devil. I love to spend other people's money. So what did you want to know about bars?"

"I thought I'd try sitting in one to see what happens, as part of my fact-finding for you."

"Sounds reasonable."

"I thought so, too, but Lucas didn't like the idea. I said I'd ask you."

"I wonder why he would be opposed?" Marcy replied thoughtfully.

Emily shrugged. "Who knows. Maybe he was dumped in one once?"

"Lucas Sheridan? Dumped?" Marcy asked skeptically. "What woman in her right mind would dump him? Even if you discount all that lovely money, he's gorgeous. The man gives me the shivers."

"Especially if he's cooking."

"He cooks?"

"I think a more accurate description would be that he sacrifices things on the altar of his ineptitude."

Marcy blinked. "Oh?"

"Yes, 'Oh.' And now that you've satisfied your curiosity, go away."

"Hospitality isn't what it used to be," Marcy grumbled as she got to her feet.

"Sleeping isn't, either." Emily walked Marcy to the door. "I'll stop by and see you next week and let you know how things are going. Goodbye."

Emily locked the door behind Marcy, yawned and then ambled back into the kitchen to get her cup of coffee. She eyed the huge Garfield clock on the wall and briefly debated going back to bed, but decided it wasn't worth the effort.

She pushed open the kitchen window and leaned out, taking a deep breath of the flower-perfumed air. She smiled as she listened to the birds chattering in the tree. It was going to be a beautiful day—clear, sunny and not oppressively hot. One of those early fall days that poets waxed lyrical about. And not only was the weather perfect, but she was going to be enjoying it with a very intriguing man.

She wandered back into her bedroom to get dressed. If she hurried, she could get all her applesauce-making equipment set up before Lucas arrived.

Emily was in the process of putting her canning jars in the dishwasher when her doorbell rang. Her muscles froze even as her heartbeat accelerated. Answering the door, she tried not to notice how enticingly the canary-yellow knit shirt revealed the breadth of Lucas's chest and seemed to darken the tan of his skin to a deep amber.

"Good morning?" he asked.

"Aren't you sure?"

"I'm sure, but you seem a little . . ." He reached out and cupped her chin in his palm, tilting her head back slightly as he studied her features.

Emily tensed against the heat radiating from his fingers.

"Distraught," he finally decided. "Did I get you up?"

Emily stepped back, breaking the unsettling physical contact. "No, that distinction belongs to Marcy. She stopped by here at six-thirty while she was out jogging."

"Six-thirty!" He winced. "On a Saturday morning? And I thought she was a friend of yours."

Emily laughed. "There are times when Marcy definitely comes under the heading With Friends Like That Who Needs Enemies." Then she picked up her purse and stepped out, locking the door behind them.

"Ah, good morning, Emily," a stick-thin woman greeted from two doors down. "Getting an early start on the day, I see. Everard and I have just had our morning constitutional." The woman gestured at the fat poodle at her feet, and then turned her attention to Lucas.

"Mrs. Kitchener, this is Lucas Sheridan. Lucas, my neighbor, Mrs. Kitchener."

"And Everard," Mrs. Kitchener added.

"Mrs. Kitchener, Everard." Lucas reached down to pat the dog.

"Don't do that!" Emily grabbed his arm and jerked it back a second before Everard's sharp white teeth closed with a snap.

"Everard!" Mrs. Kitchener sounded appalled. "You mustn't bite strangers. You might catch something." She straightened and smiled sweetly at Emily. "Have a nice day, my dear, and it was nice to meet you Mr. Sheridan." With a tug on the still-snarling dog's leash, she disappeared into her apartment.

"I think I've just been insulted. And I've always rather liked dogs."

"I'm not convinced that beast is a dog. I think in his last life he was a Tasmanian devil and he hasn't as yet shaken that reincarnation off."

"If he doesn't mend his ways, he's going to wind up in his next life very quickly. You, Emily McGregor, have a strange assortment of friends."

"Speaking of friends, I asked Marcy what she thought about us testing out a bar." Emily said.

"And?"

"And she sees no harm in it."

"Might I remind you that this is the same lady who thinks it's fine to wake you up at six-thirty on a Saturday morning."

"No, you may not." Emily pushed open her apartment-building door. She paused on the brick steps and took a deep breath. "I love fall."

"It isn't fall until September twenty-second."

"And I hate literalists." She grinned at him.

"You who make her living by teaching facts?"

"History is a whole lot more than facts!" she protested. "It's the people behind the facts that make history so fascinating. The who did what to whom and why that resulted in the action that produced the facts. It's—" She broke off as he stopped beside a bronze Porsche sports car. "Good Lord! Is that thing yours?"

"Uh-huh. Don't you approve of sports cars?"

"It's not that. It's just that we'd better take my station wagon. You don't have room for a bushel of apples."

"Probably not," Lucas conceded as he followed her over to her car. "I made out a basic list of the furniture I'll need," he told her once they'd left the parking lot. "So it shouldn't take us much time. Especially with you there to protect me from salesclerks." He gave her a conspiratorial grin, and Emily felt her stomach twist in response. She might be able to protect him from importuning salesclerks, but who was going to protect her from him?

They reached the furniture store a few minutes after it opened—a distinctive disadvantage from Lucas's point of view since it meant that virtually all the clerks were free. They had no sooner stepped into the store than they were accosted by a saleswoman who gave them a practiced smile and asked, "What may I show you today?"

"Nothing, thank you," Emily replied. "We're just looking."

"What period are you interested in?" the woman persisted.

"We favor an eclectic style, but if we should need help, we'll be sure to ask."

The woman gave Emily a frustrated smile and retreated to the front counter, where she continued to watch them.

"Very impressive," Lucas approved. "But why did you tell her we were just going to look? The whole purpose of coming this morning was to buy."

"Telling a clerk that you're just looking is a polite way of saying go away and don't bother me. Don't you ever say that to clerks?"

He frowned. "Of course not. Why would I go shopping if I didn't need to buy something?"

"Some of us have been known to shop just for the fun of it," she said dryly.

"A total waste of time. And, speaking of wasting time, we'd better move. I don't trust the way she's eyeing us. Rather like my mother used to look at me," he added absently.

"Your mother?" Emily was curious about his background.

"Everyone has one." The bleak expression on his face belied his casual words.

Emily wanted to take him in her arms and hug him. And she didn't even know why. Before she could figure out a way to probe his reaction, he gestured around the showroom and said, "Where shall we start?"

"How about with bedding, since that's the most important thing for your comfort?" she suggested.

"Yes." His husky whisper sent a shock wave of sensation through her.

Emily cleared her throat, annoyed at him and herself. She wasn't some naive young thing. She was a mature woman with a responsible job. It had been a long time since a man had been able to send her into confused retreat by a suggestive remark.

"The bedding is in the back of the store." She started through the maze of furniture only to come to a precipitous halt when she realized that Lucas was no longer with her. She turned to find him about six feet behind her, staring in rapt fascination at a seven-foot-tall armoire.

Emily retraced her steps and studied the exquisite piece of furniture. It was an Oriental design and its black lacquer finish had been elaborately decorated with stylized drawings. The armoire was a masterpiece of craftsmanship.

"What do you think?" Lucas reverently traced his finger over the gold dragon on the front.

"It's absolutely gorgeous, far too large for your apartment and—" she winced as she checked the price "—exorbitantly expensive."

He looked at her in amazement. "Economy from the woman who told me I was worth millions?"

"If you'll remember correctly, you never confirmed it."

"Consider it confirmed." He opened the doors to discover a place to put a television.

"It's still too big," Emily pointed out. "It'll dwarf your living room."

"True," he admitted and then brightened. "But I've only signed a year's lease. I told the university that if I liked teaching, then I'd accept a permanent position. If I do that, I'll build a house."

"A very big house, if this is a sample of what you like."

"This is a fantastic piece of furniture." The blond salesclerk, sensing a sale, moved in for the kill.

"We'll take it," Lucas told her. "But we aren't finished yet. We still need a few more things."

"You do?" The woman gave them a calculating look. "Perhaps I could show you—"

"Thank you, but we prefer to do our deciding alone." Emily waved off the clerk. "We feel freer to discuss things that way."

"As you wish." The woman conceded defeat. "But be sure to tell any other salesclerk who asks that Jolene is already waiting on you."

"Certainly." Lucas took Emily's arm and hastily pulled her away. "Where did you say those beds were?"

"To your right. Behind all this living-room furniture. But since we're here, why don't we get a couch and a couple of chairs?"

"Good idea." He beamed at her. "This is much easier with you."

Emily didn't quite trust his comment. "You used to run a good-size company. How can a visit to a furniture store possibly throw you?"

"Probably for the same reason that trying to run my company would throw you despite the fact that you're a highly competent teacher," he responded, mentally kicking himself for overplaying his chosen role of incompetent male. Emily might be predisposed to think of him as hopeless around a house, but she wasn't a fool. "Expertise in one field does not necessarily transfer to another."

"I guess," Emily acknowledged. "So tell me what you want in the way of a sofa?"

"Comfort first and cheerfulness second. Like..." He slowly perused the sofas on display. "That one." He started toward a nine-foot-long, contemporary piece upholstered in an eye-catching red, blue and purple Paisley print.

He sank down on it and smiled in satisfaction as the down pillows billowed around him.

"Try it." He patted the spot beside him.

Emily sat down, trying to maintain a slight distance, but the softness of the cushions defeated her. They promptly tipped her toward his much heavier body.

Emily took a deep, steadying breath that was definitely a mistake. It made her exquisitely aware of his cologne—a crisp, bracing scent that evoked images of wide-open spaces and cowboys. She pictured Lucas wearing a battered Stetson, astride a black stallion.

"You like it, too," Lucas observed, misreading the cause of her pleasure.

"Oh, yes," she agreed dreamily. "It smells—" What was it about Lucas Sheridan that so effortlessly upset her normal good sense? "It certainly is comfortable," she said.

"But?" He immediately picked up on the reservation in her voice.

"It's rather long, the vivid print is going to overwhelm your small living room. Especially when you add that armoire you just bought."

"I spent my childhood with furniture so old and shabby it didn't have any color and my entire adult life living in service flats where the dominant shade was beige. This time, I intend to splash out a little with some color."

Emily studied the bold design for a second and then commented, "That sofa isn't a splash, it's a tidal wave."

"Do you really think it's that bad?"

"It's not bad at all. And, if it makes you happy, why shouldn't you have it? You could always get a couple of chairs in a nice, retiring cream color and buy a glass coffee table to give an illusion of space."

"Good idea," he promptly agreed. "Now to the beds." He stood and, taking her hand, pulled her to her feet.

Emily shivered slightly at the latent power she could feel in him, but it was a pleasant sensation. His strength didn't threaten her; it made her feel safe, protected.

"What size bed do you want?" The salesclerk seemed to have materialized out of thin air.

"Big," Lucas answered.

"We cater to every size." She gestured toward the assortment of beds on display. "Look around and be sure to lie down and try out the various models. You can't really appreciate the difference in firmness if you don't."

"Thank you." All this talk about beds was beginning to make Emily very uneasy. "And while we're doing that, why don't you add the sofa we were looking at to his bill."

"Certainly." The woman gave her a satisfied smile and hurried away before they could change their minds.

Lucas studied the bed in front of them. "Much too small."

"It's a double and there's only one of you," Emily pointed out.

"I'm a restless sleeper, and I like to plan for all contingencies. I want something like . . . that." He started toward a larger bed farther down the line.

Emily trailed along behind him. *What contingencies?* she wondered. Did he already have a lover?

Emily fought the surge of dark emotion that flooded her thoughts. She couldn't possibly be jealous. She was just tired. Not only had she been working flat out for weeks getting ready for the start of the semester, but she'd only gotten four and a half hour's sleep last night.

"Where are you from?" Emily suddenly turned to ask him.

"San Francisco, born and bred," he muttered absently. He sat down on the mattress and bounced lightly. Then he lay back and stretched out.

As if compelled, Emily's gaze traveled the length of his body.

"Lie down beside me to make sure it's big enough, would you?" Lucas requested.

There's definitely a girlfriend, Emily concluded gloomily. Stifling a sigh, she lay down on the mattress and immediately wished she hadn't. Despite the fact that they weren't actually touching, she could feel the heat from his body seeping into hers, electrifying the fine hairs on her arms and making her muscles tighten.

"What do you think?" Lucas asked.

"That you have more than your share of the bed."

"I only have half."

"Sure—the middle half, which only leaves me with a quarter here and a quarter over there." *And a hundred percent frustrated.*

"Perhaps you should consider twin beds." The smooth voice of the clerk acted like a douse of cold water on Emily's emotions, effectively reminding her that she was in a store and in full view of anyone who cared to look.

"Absolutely not!" Lucas's response was emphatic. "We'll simply get the king-size bed instead of this queen-size one. In extra firm," he added.

What's going to have to be extra firm is my will-power, Emily reflected grimly as she got to her feet.

4

EMILY SLOWED HER station wagon to a crawl as she turned onto the dirt road.

"Good Lord! Why don't they pave this?" Lucas braced his feet against the floorboards as the car bounced over the deep ruts.

"I asked that question once and was told that they put down a couple of tons of gravel every spring." Emily gripped the steering wheel as she tried to maneuver around the worst of the chuckholes.

"And this is the fall," Lucas concluded sarcastically, rolling up his window as their wheels sent up a cloud of dust. "I'll bet the orchard's owner owns stock in a few local car-repair shops. Someone stands to make a fortune fixing suspensions and front-end alignments."

"Maybe on that expensive toy of yours, but Old Betsy here has character." Emily patted her steering wheel affectionately.

"Let's hope that all that character is firmly anchored to her frame, or Old Betsy is going to find her character along with her other assorted parts littering this cow path."

"What are you doing?" he asked as Emily carefully guided the car between two rows of trees and then cut the engine.

"Parking the car out of the way."

"There isn't a parking lot somewhere in all these trees?"

"Not really. There're a few spots up by the house, but they're always taken. This is easier. We can pick the apples, put them directly into the car and then walk up to the house and pay for them when we're done. Now, all we need to do is to pick out a good tree."

She got out of the car and looked around. Neat rows of semidwarf apple trees formed lines toward the horizon. Lucas got out her battered bushel basket and trudged after Emily as she wandered between the trees. She paused and turned to pick a large red apple from one, polished it on her jeans, and then took a bite.

Lucas watched a tiny rivulet of apple juice dribble down her chin. Her soft, red lips glistened with the juice, and he was pierced by a surge of desire so intense it shocked him. He wanted nothing more than to press his lips to hers, to taste the fruit on her lips and explore its flavor in her mouth.

Soon, he promised himself. Soon, he'd find a way to kiss her without straining the tenuous first bonds of friendship he was so carefully trying to form with her.

"Want a bite?" Emily offered him the apple.

A wicked smile curved his lips.

"Was that a Freudian slip?" Lucas deliberately bit from the exact spot where she'd been eating.

"Freudian..." Emily frowned uncomprehendingly and then grinned as his meaning became clear. "Sorry. There's no ulterior motive involved. It's an apple, plain and simple."

"There's nothing plain and simple about you, Emily McGregor. You are one very complicated lady."

Emily was wary of the gleam in his eye. She didn't want him curious about her.

"I'm not complicated about fruit," she quickly returned. "Besides, I subscribe to the Spanish version of the forbidden fruit."

"Spanish?"

"You know. That it wasn't an apple Eve gave Adam, but an orange."

"Actually, I didn't know," he said. "In fact, I've never heard of that theory."

"You haven't?" Emily blinked in surprise.

"No, I was never the least bit interested in the humanities when I was in school. I took exactly what was needed to graduate and not one course more."

"But surely you read—"

"I read technical and business journals. I never had time for anything else." He stared into the distance as if watching events long past. "When I was twelve," he continued, "my father lost his job and was out of work for the better part of a year. Things were even rougher than they normally were around our place.

"I decided then that it was never going to happen to me. That I was going to make so much money that I'd never have to worry about how I was going to pay the rent. By the time I won a scholarship to Yale, I'd realized the surest way of accomplishing that was to own my own company. And you can't build a successful company and keep it that way unless you're willing to invest all your time and energy in it. Until now, I've never had a chance to explore other interests. Old Spanish legends don't come under that heading. I prefer the concrete, like economics."

"Economics concrete?" Emily stared at him in disbelief. "Economics is one of the most *un*concrete subjects I've ever come across. No one seems to have the vaguest idea why the economy reacts the way it does. Or even why it works in the first place."

"Picky, picky." He waved off her comment. "Economics follows well-defined rules."

"You've got a lot more in common with Marcy than I originally thought," Emily observed dryly. "She thinks psychology is logical, too. Now, then—" she squinted at him in the strong sunlight "—we'd better get our apples picked or we won't be able to get them canned by this evening."

"That apple we just sampled tasted good. Why not pick them?"

"Because it was a Red Delicious."

"So?" Lucas remembered just in time that he wasn't supposed to know which apples were for eating and which were for cooking.

"You can't cook Red Delicious apples."

"Who says we can't?" Lucas questioned as he trailed along behind her.

"That basic cookbook you're going to buy says so." She paused to check an apple hanging on a tree.

"Hey, you two, that's our tree! We're going to pick it just as soon as we finish over here," a belligerent-sounding woman yelled down the row.

"Sorry," Emily said, moving away.

"That's ridiculous," Lucas protested. "Do you realize how many bushels of apples there must be on each of those trees? She can't possibly use all those apples."

"Probably not, but it's not worth fighting about."

"Isn't it?" Lucas eyed her serene features. "Don't you consider standing up for yourself worth fighting about?"

"That rather depends. Like most people, I'll fight if it's important enough to me, but letting that woman hog a few trees simply isn't that important. Not when there are so many others."

"I suppose. But her attitude still grates."

"That's because you're a very competitive person," she said slowly. "And then again, maybe it's simply the difference between our sexes."

"Emily, there's nothing simple about the difference between our sexes. It's fascinating, perhaps. Definitely absorbing. Maybe even awe inspiring. But most emphatically, not simple."

Heat raced through Emily at the sudden husky tone of his voice. It was as if his words were creating a wall around them, isolating them. No, she resolutely rejected what he was doing to her. She couldn't think of him in sexual terms. The problem was, how was she going to stop herself? Lucas Sheridan was undoubtedly the most masculine man she'd ever met, and it wasn't just his looks; it was some illusive quality that he wore with all the assurance of a conqueror.

If only— She forced herself to concentrate on the question at hand. "We're here—" She winced at the slight unsteadiness of her voice. "We're here to pick apples, not to indulge in a lot of idle chitchat."

"So we are." Lucas immediately backed off. He wanted to slip past her guard, which meant not making her nervous. "And if we aren't picking Red Delicious apples, which ones are we picking?"

"The Idareds on this tree should make good sauce." She looked around. "And no one seems to have staked a claim to it yet."

"I'm here, lady," a thin voice floated down from above.

Emily jumped at the unexpected sound and looked up. She discovered a small boy perched on a branch two feet above their heads. His hair was full of twigs and one rosy cheek was smeared with dirt. He'd tucked his brilliant red jersey into his jeans and then stuffed the apples he'd picked inside, making him look as if he were the victim of some exotic disease.

Emily swallowed the smile that threatened and said, "I'm so sorry. I didn't realize this tree was already occupied."

"S'okay, lady," he mumbled around a mouthful of apple. He swallowed and then continued. "There's plenty here to share. My name's Harry, and I'm only picking the biggest. You two can have the rest."

"Thank you." Lucas set the bushel basket down between them and began to inspect the apples on the lower branches. Emily wasn't so discriminating. She simply began to pick from the branch nearest her.

"Hey, lady?"

"I'm Emily."

"Emily?" the boy repeated dubiously. "I don't think I'm supposed to call old people by their first names."

"It doesn't bother me, but you can use Miss McGregor."

"Like the farmer in *Peter Rabbit*?" the boy chortled gleefully. "Do you put people in pots?"

Emily laughed. "So far I've managed to resist the temptation. Lucas—" He was staring up through the tree with a calculating expression.

Emily followed his gaze, but could see nothing out of the ordinary except, of course, Harry.

"What's the matter?" she finally asked.

"The kid's right. The apples really are bigger up there."

Emily shrugged. "It's probably because they get more sunlight. Or maybe it's simply a case of the grass being greener on the other side."

"They're bigger," Lucas repeated stubbornly. "Those are the ones we ought to be picking. Are there any ladders around?"

"The owner usually scatters some around the orchard for people to use, but why bother? The smaller ones on the lower branches will do."

"But those up there are bigger," he insisted.

"But what difference does that make? All I intend to do is to reduce them to sauce anyway."

"I guess you're right," he said reluctantly. He began to pick the apples he could reach, all the while casting longing glances up at the bigger ones.

Emily covertly watched him as she worked. His streak of competitiveness was apparent. He would automatically go after the best—whether or not it was logical to do so. Was this a conscious thing? Or was it such an ingrained habit that he didn't even realize he was doing it?

Was it possible that he saw her as a challenge? She knew that for a lot of men, possessing her beauty was an end in itself; that they didn't care about the personality behind the face. But that shouldn't be true with Lucas. Because of his wealth, beautiful women certainly wouldn't be a novelty to him. In the relatively narrow world of the university, she might be unique, but in San Francisco she would merely be one of many beautiful women. Comforted by her reasoning, Emily cheerfully went back to picking apples. With the two of them working, the basket filled quickly.

"Can we round the top of the bushel off with apples?" Lucas asked.

"Within reason." Emily watched in amusement as he carefully piled apples in the center of the basket. "However, you are fast approaching the limits of reason."

"You think so?" Lucas eyed his handiwork critically and then added one more apple to the exact center. "If they're selling a bushel, then it seems to me that everything you could get into a bushel would be okay."

"It's what it seems to the orchard's owner that counts. Chances are he'll—"

"Hey, Miss McGregor?"

Emily had forgotten Harry was still in the tree. "Yes?"

"Can you see my mother?"

"What does she look like?" Emily asked.

"Like my mother!"

Emily glanced around the orchard. There was an elderly couple a few trees down and a teenage boy in the row beside them. While she could hear other voices, she couldn't actually see anyone else.

"I can't see her. Perhaps I could help instead?" Emily offered.

"You?" Harry looked dubious.

Lucas leaned up against the gnarled tree trunk and smiled reassuringly at the child. "Why don't you come down from your perch and we can go look for your mother together?"

"'Cause I can't! I'm stuck. My shirt's caught, and if I rip it, my mom'll be real mad."

"Not to worry," Lucas said. "I'll have you free in a jiffy."

Harry brightened. "Are you a fireman?"

"Naw. You only need a fireman for cats. Now hold still. I'm going to climb up and help you down, okay?"

Without waiting for an answer, Lucas grabbed the lowest branch and swung himself up into the tree.

Emily watched in fascination as his movements made the powerful muscles of his thighs bulge against the worn denim of his jeans. Lucas really was in superb physical shape, she reflected, listening as he talked to Harry. It was obvious from the soothing cadence of his voice that he liked children, and Emily felt a piercing surge of sadness over her sterility. Somehow, the very perfection of the autumn day made her grief all the more potent, intensifying the contrast between what was and what could never be.

"There you are, Harry. All clear. You climb down first, and I'll follow."

Emily saw one small skinny leg emerge from the leafy canopy. Reaching up, she steadied Harry as he cautiously inched down the tree trunk.

"If you'll wait until we put the apples in the car, we'll help you find your mother," Emily said.

"Naw." Harry rubbed a dirt-streaked hand across his dripping nose. "If'n you did that, then Mom, she'd think I'd been lost and she'd never let me out of her sight ever again."

"But—"

"Thanks, mister!" Harry shouted up at Lucas. "I gotta go now." With a final wave, he raced off between the rows of apple trees.

Emily watched him disappear. She might be lucky enough to have a little boy like that, except for—

"What's wrong?" Lucas dropped to the ground beside her.

"Nothing."

You mean, nothing that you're willing to tell me about, Lucas thought, inexplicably annoyed by the idea. He didn't want Emily shutting him out. Even less did he want to see her hurting. He wanted to make everything right in her world—which would be impossible if she refused to confide in him.

Leaning over, he lightly brushed his lips against her slightly parted mouth.

Emily trembled, then swayed toward him. Her involuntary movement instantly shattered Lucas's intention to keep it casual. Unable to resist, he pressed his lips harder. The musky, sun-warmed aroma of her skin drowned out the voice of sanity, which was urging caution.

No! Lucas reined in his growing desire with an effort that left him feeling painfully deprived. But he couldn't risk pushing her too far, too fast. He slowly raised his head.

Emily forced open her heavy eyelids and looked at him. The light streaming down through the leaves gilded his dark brown hair with reddish highlights.

"Why did you do that?" She voiced her thoughts aloud, and then winced at the sound of her impossibly naive words.

To her relief, Lucas appeared to take her words at face value. He gave her a rueful grin and replied, "Because men are opportunists at heart."

Emily laughed, responding to his lighthearted expression. "I'm not so sure all men have hearts."

"I refuse to get into a philosophical discussion on such a beautiful day."

"In that case, there's nothing left to do but to get these apples back to my place and process them. You take that handle and I'll get the other one. That way we can hold it level between us."

"Careful," he warned as she lifted her side too quickly. "They'll spill."

"One of the dangers of overconsumption."

"One should always maximize the amount one receives from each investment. Be careful of the ruts in the path," he added as they started back.

"Tell me—" she remembered her earlier reservations about his competitiveness "—does that philosophy extend to women?"

Lucas glanced at her speculatively and asked, "In what sense?"

"Do you always try to get the maximum out of every relationship you have?"

Lucas frowned as if seriously considering her question. "Actually, I'm not sure. There haven't been enough relationships for me to generalize."

"You're telling me that a man in your financial position didn't have a full social life? I remember reading once that the most potent aphrodisiac for women is power and the second is money. You had both."

"True," he admitted. "But I wasn't kidding when I said that making a fortune from virtually nothing takes years of working sixteen-hour days. Of subordinating everything to your goal. And that includes your personal life."

"But you're a normal, healthy male and..." She paused as she realized where her curiosity was leading her. Lucas was being amazingly open with her, but what she was asking was really none of her business—even if she was consumed with the desire to know.

"Make no mistake about it, Emily." He gave her a look that stopped her. "I have all the normal masculine responses to a desirable woman. I didn't say there had been no women. Simply that there had been very few.

"Tell me," he continued at her disbelieving look, "do you have all the desires of a normal, healthy woman?"

"Well, yes. I suppose so," she said cautiously, starting to have second thoughts about where the conversation might be leading.

"And have you engaged in a series of affairs to indulge them?"

"Of course not!"

"Then why would you assume that I would?"

"Because men—" Emily paused in dismay as she realized just what she was saying. She was guilty of sexual stereotyping. "Sorry. I seem to have been guilty of a spot of sexual bias, there."

"And stupidity, too." His smile robbed the words of their sting. "Anyone who engages in promiscuous sex these days runs a very real risk of winding up with AIDS."

"True," Emily conceded. "We—" She paused as she caught sight of a flash of a red T-shirt to her right. "Say, isn't that our erstwhile Tarzan?"

Lucas turned and then chuckled as he saw Harry talking to two little girls. "And that must be Mom chasing that toddler."

"Toddlers. There's another in the grass behind Harry. I'll bet both of them belong to her."

"Probably. They all look alike. Don't you like children?" He wondered if he'd misjudged her reaction to Harry.

"Of course, I like children." *Even if I can't have any myself.* She tried the words out in her mind, but somehow they seemed too bald. "I just don't think it's a good idea for a woman to have five kids in what appears to be as many years," she finally said. "Not only is it hard on her body, but the kids would never have a chance to get their mother to themselves."

Lucas remained silent for a few minutes and then, to Emily's relief, changed the subject. "If I remember correctly, the car is a few rows to our left."

"Right," she replied.

"Right as in not left or right as in okay?"

She chuckled. "Right as in okay."

At the car they loaded the basket in the rear. "Why don't you stay here with the apples while I walk up to the house and pay for them?" Lucas suggested. "That way we won't have to lock the car up."

"Sure." Emily leaned up against car door, enjoying the soft, drowsy September air. The peace of the day was rudely shattered as a car going far too fast for the orchard's primitive conditions skidded off the side of the road into the shallow ditch in front of her.

"Damn fool idiot!" An elderly couple emerged from the trees behind Emily. "This orchard is crawling with kids, and he drives like an escapee from a California freeway," the man said.

"Now, Daniel, don't swear," his wife chided.

"I think we're safe for the moment." Emily watched as the young man in the car revved his engine and his back tires spun ineffectively. "He appears to be stuck."

"Good." Daniel looked at the angry-looking driver in disgust. "Serves him right."

"Now, dear, we really ought to see if he needs any help," his wife said. "He might not be able to get out on his own."

"We should be so lucky."

"Now, dear, we must take the charitable view."

"There's no must about it." Daniel turned to Emily, who was trying hard not to laugh. "What do you think, miss?"

"Well . . ." Emily weighed what she should say. Daniel didn't look strong enough to be pushing cars. In fact, she doubted if she, Daniel and his wife together could push the car back on the road, but she didn't want to tell Daniel that.

"See." Daniel turned triumphantly to his wife. "She agrees with me. She's just too polite to say so."

"Actually, tempting though it is to let him stew in his own juice, I suppose we ought to ask if he wants us to get the orchard's owner to bring a tractor to pull him out."

The old woman smiled approvingly at Emily. "I knew I was right. Go ask the boy if he wants us to walk up to the house and get him help, Daniel."

"Go see if he needs help," the old man mimicked. "If we're dumb enough to get him out of that ditch, we'll be the ones who'll be needing help." He stalked across the narrow dirt road and had almost reached the car when the driver suddenly floored his accelerator. The engine raced and the rear wheels spun for a second before they caught on a tuft of grass. With a roar that sounded ominous, the car careened backward, straight at Daniel.

Emily screamed. The young driver looked behind him and saw Daniel standing frozen in the road. Panicking, he swung the wheel of his car to the right and clipped the old man in the leg, sending him to the ground.

Emily raced to Daniel, trailed by his sobbing wife.

"Emily!" She heard her name being called in a voice she barely recognized, but she was too worried about Daniel to respond.

"Emily, what the hell happened?" Hard hands grabbed her by the shoulder and spun her around. She found herself staring into Lucas's blazing eyes. His face was set in taut lines.

"It's not me. It's him." Emily reached for Daniel, but Lucas grabbed her hand.

"Don't touch him," Lucas ordered.

"It wasn't my fault." In his fear, the driver of the car sounded very young. "That old man just walked in back of me."

Lucas cut him off: "I'm not the least bit interested in assigning blame. Get up to the house and tell them to call the police and an ambulance right now."

"Police!" The young man turned chalk white. "But—"

"Now!" Lucas's authoritative voice sliced into his protest.

Obediently he turned and sprinted toward the house while Lucas leaned over and gently searched for a pulse in the old man's neck.

"Please, God," the old woman muttered, "if you'll just let him live, I promise I'll never make him do anything he doesn't want to again."

"You won't grumble when I have a can of beer with the ten o'clock news?" Daniel's voice was weak but teasing.

"Oh, Daniel, you're alive!" The woman turned even whiter, closed her eyes, and pitched forward in a dead faint.

Lucas caught her before she hit the ground.

"Emily, open the back door of that kid's car. I'll lay her across the seat, and she can go in the ambulance with her husband."

"I don't need any ambulance," Daniel protested. "All I lost was my dignity and some skin on my leg."

"I think you must have smacked your head when you were knocked down. You were out for a minute," Emily said.

"Nonsense." He sounded stronger. "How's Martha? She always did take things too much to heart."

"She just fainted. She'll be okay."

"I'm going to—"

"Lie exactly where you are." There was a thread of steel in Lucas's voice. "You're probably right that you're simply shaken up, but on the off chance that something is broken, we'll play it safe. If not for your sake, then for Martha's. She depends on you, you know."

"She's a fine woman," Daniel said gruffly. "A bit of a do-gooder, but a fine woman."

Just then, a jeep came roaring down the road and shrieked to a halt in front of them. The owner of the orchard vaulted out. "I've called an ambulance. They said they'll be here in a few minutes. How is he?" He gestured toward Daniel.

"I'm not dead yet, young man!" Daniel snapped. "And there's no need for you all to sit here and stare at me like I was the guest of honor at a wake." He glared at Emily.

"Sorry." Emily giggled with sheer relief.

"You can leave him to me," the owner assured Lucas. "I was a paramedic in Nam. I'll make sure he doesn't move."

"All right." Lucas got to his feet. "The less people milling around, the better. His wife fainted. She's in the car."

"I saw what happened," Emily told the owner. "If the police should want to talk to me, my name is Emily McGregor. I teach at the university." She gently touched the old man's shoulder. "Good luck, Daniel."

"Don't worry." Daniel gave her a rueful grin. "I'll be fine once I get back home."

"I hope he's right," Emily said as she followed Lucas over to her car.

"He will be." Lucas sounded confident, and Emily believed him. "But just to put your mind at rest, we'll call the hospital when we get back and make sure."

5

"ARE THEY ALL RIGHT?" Emily demanded when Lucas hung up the phone.

"The hospital says they're fine. Daniel was treated for cuts and abrasions and Martha's fully recovered. Their son is coming to pick them up and take them home."

Lucas watched as the tenseness faded from her face and her mouth resumed its normal soft lines, wondering why she had been so worried. It was as if she were in the grip of an underlying tension, and whenever anything happened, it tapped into that tension, magnifying her reaction. Somehow he had to get close enough to her to gain her trust so that she'd tell him what was bothering her. And that would take time. Time and patience. He stifled a sigh. He didn't want to be patient; he wanted to take her in his arms, kiss her senseless and then make love to her until she couldn't think of anything but him. That tantalizing kiss they'd shared earlier hadn't appeased his desire; it had made him realize just what he'd been missing all his life.

He was coming to suspect that Emily was exactly what he'd always hoped to find. She'd simply appeared on the scene a couple of years before he'd planned to go looking for her. He grinned wolfishly. He was nothing if not adaptable. Fifteen years of successfully competing in business had taught him the necessity of grabbing an advantage when it appeared because it might not come around again.

Bless Marcy and her study, he thought as he followed Emily into the kitchen, his eyes on the movement of her trim hips beneath the faded denim of her jeans. Fate had certainly given him an opportunity, and he had no intention of wasting it.

Emily peered into the huge pot steaming on her stove. Picking up a fork, she stabbed a few apple quarters and then nodded in satisfaction.

Lucas leaned over her shoulder to see what she was doing, and Emily tensed. "I still think you ought to have at least taken the seeds out," Lucas remarked skeptically.

"Don't worry about it. The strainer will take care of them." She gestured toward the shiny aluminum device she'd screwed to the edge of her counter earlier that morning.

To her relief, Lucas went to inspect the strainer—she found it much easier to concentrate when he wasn't quite so close.

"How does this thing work?" He looked down into the oversize funnel at the top.

"With a minimum of effort." Emily ladled partially cooked chunks of apple into the funnel, set a bowl under the spout and then gave the handle a whirl. Squashed apple emerged from the spout while seeds, peels and stems came out the back.

"Hey, that's fantastic!" Lucas's eyes lit up with all the enthusiasm of a small boy presented with a new toy. "Let me." He turned the handle and watched, enthralled, as the applesauce poured out in a slow steady stream. "What do we do now?"

Emily ladled more of the steaming apple chunks into the funnel. "After we get all the apples squashed, we heat them to boiling, fill the canning jars, boil those in a water bath, and then we're done."

"Hmm." Lucas studied the steady stream of applesauce pouring into the bowl. He'd never canned before and he was finding it fascinating. "May I have some of this?"

"Sure, if you want. What are you going to do with it?"

"Make apple butter. It shouldn't be that hard," he said absently.

Emily barely suppressed a shudder at the thought. "You can take a few jars home with you and make it there. You can let me know how it turns out," she added.

"Better still, I'll bring you some and you can taste for yourself," he offered, breathing a sigh of relief that she had assumed his comment on how easy it would be stemmed from ignorance and not from knowledge. He frowned inwardly. He didn't like having to watch what he said to Emily. He would have infinitely preferred to be completely open with her, but he couldn't be. Not yet.

Emily secretly watched as the muscles in his arms rippled with his every turn of the handle. What would it feel like to have those arms wrapped around her, holding her crushed against him?

"I need more." Lucas's husky voice filtered into her mind.

"Definitely," she murmured as a faint pink flush skated across her cheekbones. *Much more . . .*

"Emily, is the steam getting to you?" Lucas's worried tone jerked her back to reality and she took a deep breath, fighting her way out of the sensual haze.

"Umm, no. I'm okay." She used the mundane task of adding apples to the funnel to give herself time to control her wayward emotions. What was it about Lucas Sheridan that seemed to send her into a dreamlike state at the drop of a hat? Unfortunately, she had no answer and decided to worry about that later, when she was away from Lucas's distracting presence.

By five o'clock the jars of applesauce were cooling in neat rows on her counter and her kitchen had been returned to its normally pristine state.

She poured out two mugs of coffee, handed one to Lucas and headed into the living room. "Do you have to leave at any particular time?" she asked, telling herself that she wasn't prying into his personal life. She was simply trying to figure out how long they had to work on their research plans for Marcy's study.

"Shortly." Lucas set his drink on the coffee table and plopped down on her sofa. He stretched his long legs out in front of him, and again Emily found her gaze caught and held by the movement of their powerful muscles.

"Dean Goodman is having a barbecue for the faculty in the School of Business tonight."

Emily sank into the armchair across from him, resisting her initial impulse to sit beside him on the sofa. The very strength of that impulse was the reason she ignored it.

"It should be a good chance for me to meet some of my colleagues."

And for them to meet you. Especially that rapacious, man-hungry barracuda known as Tricia Corey, who taught accounting and had already been through innumerable lovers and three husbands, and who made no bones about the fact that she was in search of husband number four. Emily studied Lucas carefully, trying to assess his appeal to the average woman. It was enormous, she decided. Not only was he a very good-looking man, but he was also very wealthy. Tricia would think she'd died and gone to heaven.

"What's the matter?" Lucas frowned at her abstracted expression. "Is there something I should know about Dean Goodman's parties?"

"Not really." She forced a smile. "You should enjoy yourself and, as you say, it'll be an excellent chance for you to get to know the rest of the faculty in your school. Make sure you meet Bob Jeffries. He's an economist with some fascinating ideas on the restructuring of the country's tax system."

"I will, but I still want to know why you were looking at me as if you'd never seen me before."

Emily mixed part of the truth with a plausible lie. "I was thinking about how you look, and I was wondering if anyone's done a study on attractive men like Marcy's."

"I vaguely remember reading a few years back about a study on height. The article said that the overwhelming majority of upper-level managers were over six feet, but that it didn't hold true for the heads of companies."

"I'll have to mention that to Marcy. It would be interesting if she could compare what she discovers with what's been found out about the impact of men's physical appearances."

"Men don't judge on appearance," Lucas said.

"Lucas Sheridan, that's a barefaced lie and you know it!" she retorted. "Sometimes that's the only thing men judge by."

"I'm talking about business."

"So am I."

"What would you know about business?" he scoffed.

"Don't kid yourself, my friend. Education is big business. It's just a lot harder to judge what's being produced."

"We'll see. I spoke to my friend who owns the plastics factory south of town, and he said that you could be the receptionist two weeks from Thursday."

"I only have one class on Thursdays, so I should be able to get someone to cover it for me with no problem," she replied.

"If we schedule your stint as a receptionist for then, and return something to the department store this coming Saturday, we can fit in trying to get a table in a crowded restaurant the following Saturday. That is, if it's a home football weekend?"

"It is," she said grimly. "The dates are indelibly engraved in my mind."

"Why? Do you have tickets?"

"No. What I have is brains. One tries to keep a low profile on football weekends. The traffic increases a thousandfold, the stores are jammed, and literally scores of kids and a few so-called adults get bombed out of their minds and then take to the roads in cars. Believe me, it's much safer to stay at home."

Lucas smiled at her. "Don't worry. I'll protect you."

He probably could, at that. He exuded the kind of authority that would give pause to even the most exuberant of partyers.

"Why don't I see if I can get tickets to the game and we could do this right," he suggested.

"That, sir, is a contradiction in terms."

"Nonsense. You just haven't had anyone explain the game to you. Football is a microcosm of life."

"Only if you live in a war zone!"

"You'll see," he insisted with a confidence that amused her; Lucas was definitely not used to people who said no.

"You certainly will see." She smiled at him. "Now, then, enough of our basic philosophical differences. Let's see if your jars of applesauce are cool enough for you to move. You don't want to be late for your barbecue."

"Say—" Lucas looked thoughtful "—would you like to show me how to barbecue something?"

Emily gave him a horrified look. "Let you loose around live coals! Not while I'm in full possession of my faculties. We'll stick to the stove."

"Why don't you give me a cooking lesson this Saturday after the department-store experiment? We could come back here, and you could show me how to do a simple dinner."

"We'll have your cooking lesson at your apartment," she said emphatically. "There's no way you're going to stick me with the disastrous results."

"My place, then." He smiled, sending a wave of anticipation through her—a sense of anticipation that grew during the following week to the extent that Emily began to feel distinctly uneasy about the way Lucas was infiltrating her thoughts.

"SORRY, I'M LATE, Emily." Lucas dropped into the seat opposite her in the department store's tearoom. "I stopped by my office to pick up some papers, and ran into one of my students. The poor kid has an outsize case of homesickness, so I spent a few minutes talking to him. I'll have to see if I can get him and a couple of others working on a short-term project for me. That would give him a chance to make a few friends in class."

Emily studied the absorbed expression on his face. A melting feeling of tenderness filled her. Not many professors cared enough about their students to try to solve their personal problems.

"You are definitely one of the good Lord's better attempts at creation, Lucas Sheridan."

Lucas blinked, looking at her in surprise. "Why? Because I was late?"

"No, because of why you were late. Far too many teachers around this place see their classes as a whole. They don't concern themselves with the individual members of those classes, let alone worry if they're happy."

"Don't try to turn me into a saint," he said seriously. "When I take on a job, I consider all the aspects of it, and delivering the lecture is only one aspect of teaching. If the student's emotional life is all screwed up, he's not going to learn. And speaking of learning, what are we hoping to learn today? Besides the fact that you look unbelievably gorgeous."

His gaze traveled over the elegant tumble of ebony curls framing her perfectly made-up face. "I wouldn't have believed it possible, but that blue dress makes your eyes even bluer and—" he leaned closer and sniffed "—you smell like an exotic flower and you feel—" he traced over her bare forearm with a questing finger "—you feel warm and infinitely desirable."

"Thank you." Her voice cracked, but she hurriedly controlled it and went on, hoping he hadn't noticed. "But touch doesn't count in this study. All Marcy gets is auditory and visual reactions."

"Just as well." To her relief, he leaned back in his chair. "Exactly how do you plan to do this?"

Emily took a small sack with the store's distinctive logo on it out of the oversize brown shopping bag at her feet. "I'm going to try to return this." She took out a futuristic-looking chrome figurine about twelve inches high. "I bought two of these yesterday when the sale started."

Lucas frowned and poked the figurine with a disdainful finger. "I can understand why you'd want to return it. What I can't understand is why you bought it in the first place."

Emily shrugged. "I had to have something to return. Besides, if they won't take them back, I can give one to the head of our department as a Christmas present."

Lucas laughed and the warm, happy sound soothed away all the little aggravations she'd encountered on her way downtown. "My God, it's true," he said.

"What's true?" she asked in bemusement, her attention focused on the laugh lines at the corners of his eyes.

"That a woman's vengeance is a terrible thing."

"It sure is. So you'd better watch yourself."

He chuckled. "Seems to me I'd do better to watch you." He looked longingly at her half-full cup of coffee, then around the crowded room for a waitress. There wasn't one to be seen. "I don't suppose you'd share a bit of caffeine, would you?" he asked hopefully.

"Sharing is undoubtedly the only way you'll get any." She pushed her cup toward him. "I swear the service in this place gets worse every time I come in. I don't know why they don't just put in some vending machines and be done with it."

Lucas took a healthy swallow of the lukewarm drink. "Thanks. I needed that. So, what else is in that thing?" He indicated the bulky shopping bag.

"My costume. I talked to my friend in the theater department yesterday, and she gave me some great tips and loaned me some props."

"Dark glasses?" he guessed.

"Tinted dark yellow with oversize, bulky frames. How'd you guess?"

"Because your eyes are the most beautiful thing about you," he explained. "The expression in them is constantly shifting—like a kaleidoscope. At the moment, they're gleaming with anticipation."

"Oh," Emily said blankly, uncertain how to respond. Any other man, and she'd have thought that he was trying to flirt with her, but with Lucas she wasn't so sure. His comment had been delivered in an almost-detached manner, as if he were stating an indisputable fact, not paying her a compliment.

"Exactly what is my part in trying to unload this—" he gestured disparagingly toward the figurine "—thing?"

"Your job will be to observe the clerk's reaction from the first moment he sees me until I leave, and to provide a distraction if anything goes wrong. Okay?"

"No problem. And I'm to stay there while you get into your disguise?"

"Yes. I'll use the ladies' room, put on my disguise and come back. Then we'll go through the whole thing again. After which we can go over to your apartment and you can have your cooking lesson. I put the ingredients for chicken Veronica in a cooler in my car."

"Chicken who?" he asked, feeling that it was safe to assume that the average man wouldn't know what the dish was.

"Veronica. It has green grapes in it. Haven't you ever had it before?"

"Nope," he lied. "The only chicken I know by name is the Colonel's."

"You need your horizons expanded. Now, then," she continued briskly, "to our battle stations. I'll give you a five-minute head start and then I'll come up."

Actually, it was almost fifteen minutes later before she arrived. She'd run into a friend from the history department who was on maternity leave. In response to Emily's social query about her health, the woman had launched into a list of complaints ranging from the fact that she hadn't wanted another child, how her figure was never going to be the same again, through how expensive setting up a nursery was, and ending with how she couldn't sleep nights because of the baby's movements.

It had been all Emily could do to politely sympathize when she would have endured any discomfort and would have traded every penny in her healthy investment portfolio to be carrying a child. After her friend had finally exhausted her list of complaints and gotten into the elevator, it had taken Emily a few minutes to force her sense of frustration and despair at the unfairness of it all to the back of her mind. Finally, when she felt in control of her emotions again, she continued on to the store's offices.

Emily immediately spotted Lucas sitting on a sofa facing the Returns desk. Emily ignored the totally irrational frisson of isolation she felt when he ignored her arrival, telling herself that she was being ridiculous. Of course, he was ignoring her. That was what he was supposed to be doing.

She took a deep breath and, using the slow, seductive walk that she'd spent her teenage years perfecting, approached the desk.

Lucas clenched his teeth together and forced himself to relax. Where had she learned to walk like that? She was a moving enticement to any male who saw her. Not that it was going to do them any good. Emily was his. She just didn't know it yet. Emily was perfect. All he had to do was to convince her of that fact.

He redirected his attention to the youngish man behind the Returns desk. Lucas watched in annoyance as his eyes lit up like a hundred-watt light bulb at the sight of Emily. The man surreptitiously straightened his tie and ran his hand over his hair.

"Excuse me, Mr. Lane—" Emily read his name off the plaque on his desk "—but could you possibly help me?" She gave him the full benefit of her smile.

"It'd be my pleasure," the man enthused. "Won't you sit down."

Emily gracefully sank into the chair in front of his desk and crossed her legs, purposefully allowing her narrow skirt to inch up her thighs.

Emily could almost hear the man's increased heart rate. She could also feel a strange prickly sensation between her shoulder blades. Telling herself she was being fanciful, she dismissed the unsettling sensation and concentrated on the salivating Mr. Lane.

"You see, Mr. Lane, it's this little sculpture." She set the statuette on his desk.

"Yes?" he asked encouragingly, barely glancing at it.

"I thought I liked it when I bought it on sale yesterday." She sighed. "But when I got home, I decided it just wasn't me."

"I should say not," he agreed in heartfelt tones.

"So I'd really appreciate it if I could return it." She gave him a hopeful look.

"Yes, of course you can," he instantly replied, ignoring store policy. Picking up a return slip, he looked at her and said, "If you'll just give me your name, address and telephone number for our records."

"Marcy Handley, and my number is 555-6281," Emily lied. If she read that gleam in his eye correctly, that phone number was for himself, and she had no intention of fending him off when he called. Marcy was the one who wanted the information; she could deal with him.

"Would an in-store credit voucher do?"

"A credit voucher's fine," Emily said, not wanting to wait while he got the refund. The exercise was leaving a bad taste in her mouth. She didn't like using her attractiveness as a weapon, and that's what she was doing. Even if Mr. Lane was a willing victim.

"There you are." He handed her the pink credit voucher and stood. "I'll walk you down to the elevator."

"Oh, that's all right," Emily told him. "I wouldn't dream of putting you to the trouble."

"No trouble at all. We here at Winthrops believe in the personal touch."

"Say, mister," Lucas's voice interrupted, "does this store have a sporting-goods department?"

Emily breathed an involuntary sigh of relief at Lucas's timely intervention.

"Thanks again, Mr. Lane," Emily said, and beat a hasty retreat down the hall while Lucas successfully detained him.

6

EMILY LOOKED AROUND the lounge of the ladies' room
in dismay. It was jammed with women taking a break
from their shopping. She'd forgotten just how busy it
could be on a Saturday afternoon.

"Hello, Dr. McGregor. Would you like to sit down?"
A nervous-looking young woman half rose from her
seat.

"No, thank you—" Emily searched her memory and
was able to put a name to the face "—Melissa."

Melissa gave her a half smile that was clearly di-
vided between pleasure that her history professor remembered her from two years ago and worry as to why
she should have.

Emily moved through the lounge and into the bath-
rooms. She only had to wait a few minutes to get into
a stall. Carefully maneuvering her oversize bag in with
her, she closed the metal door, locked it and then hung
the bag on the hook on the back of the door. It was a
tight squeeze.

Ignoring her discomfort, she pulled out the latex
bodysuit and the grayish-beige dress she'd borrowed
from the theater department and hung them on top of
her shopping bag. She slipped out of the outfit she was
wearing, wincing when she jabbed herself in the leg on
the toilet-paper holder on the left side of the stall. She

rubbed the reddening spot as she stuffed her blue dress into the shopping bag.

Emily shook out the bodysuit and inspected it, making sure the adjustable panels that were going to add fifty pounds to her figure were all properly inflated. Satisfied, she braced herself against the door and slowly inched her way into the suit. It was a slow, tortuous process—like trying to fit into a dress that was two sizes too small.

Emily shoved her arms into the suit's short sleeves and shrugged it up over her shoulders, wiggling slightly to try to make it fit more comfortably. Unfortunately, her movement brought her left hip in contact with the toilet-paper holder. Emily felt the sharp jab a second before she heard the ominous hiss of escaping air.

"Damn!" She twisted her head around, trying to see how much damage had been done, but she couldn't accurately judge in the confined space. The hissing finally stopped and Emily lightly ran her hand over her left hip and then over the right one, which was still inflated. The left side was definitely smaller. She sighed. There wasn't much she could do about it. She had no materials to repair the suit and even if she did, she doubted that she could have done it in this cramped space.

Ah, well, she thought, reaching for the dress, no one ever claimed that the price of knowledge came easy. Hopefully the bulk of the dress's material would hide part of her problem and as for the rest—she'd simply have to be careful to keep her back to Mr. Lane. Emily slipped the beige dress over her head, twitched it into place and then fastened its large pearl buttons. She

belted the fake lizard-skin belt around her waist—
which, thanks to the bodysuit, was now a good ten
inches larger—and smoothed the material over her
breasts, which had also miraculously grown, again
courtesy of the theater department. Emily stifled a giggle. For the first time in her life she was amply en-
dowed, and she found it a novel experience.

Someone bumping up against the stall door reminded Emily how long she'd been there, and she hastily gathered up her possessions and exited.

The woman waiting to use the stall barely gave her
a glance. Emily walked over to the sinks and took her
makeup kit out of the shopping bag. After carefully
creaming off her normal makeup, she pulled her long
curls back into a bun so tight that it seemed to pull the
corners of her eyes back. Releasing it ever so slightly,
she secured it with a rubber band and then anchored it
to the back of her head in a bun. A quick dusting of
powder dulled her hair's normal healthy sheen and
faded its rich color. Opening the liquid makeup, she
proceeded to apply it to her face. Its natural glow was
quickly drowned in a sallow tinge that made her look
like a recovering jaundice victim. Emily twisted her
head to one side to make sure that she'd applied it
evenly and then added a liberal coating of a garish,
bright orange lipstick. The final touch was a pair of
glasses with yellow-tinted lenses to hide her eyes.

Emily stepped back a pace and studied her reflection
with interest. It was amazing what fifty extra pounds
and all the wrong colors could do for a person. Or,
more accurately, *to* a person.

"Excuse me?" A middle-aged woman who'd been repairing her lipstick at the end of the counter spoke up. "Are you aware of the fact that your left hip is smaller than your right?"

Emily turned, wincing at the sight in the mirror. It was every bit as bad as she'd feared. She gave the woman a warm smile that not even the wrong-color lipstick could dim and said, "Would you believe I tried liposuction and it failed?"

"Possibly." The woman smiled back. "There's certainly nothing wrong with your imagination. But may I give you a piece of advice?"

"Be my guest."

"Don't smile. Even in that disguise, you look great when you smile."

"Thanks, I'll remember that. Hopefully I'll get better as I go along."

"No, my dear. You're getting worse as you go along. I saw you when you came in. Good luck."

"Thank you." Emily hurried back to the business offices, eager to get this over with.

The Returns clerk was still behind his desk. He glanced up as she entered the reception area and his gaze skidded over her with a total lack of interest.

Emily glanced at Lucas and watched in wry appreciation as his eyes first widened in disbelief at the sight of her, then narrowed as he fought to suppress the laughter that threatened to erupt.

She stopped in front of the desk and waited for the clerk to acknowledge her. It took over a minute before he finally looked up. He gave her a perfunctory smile that could have been measured in microseconds and clipped out, "May I help you?"

"Yes." Emily pulled out the twin to the sculpture she'd returned a few minutes earlier. "I bought this yesterday and when I got it home it just didn't fit in with my living room. So I want to return it."

"Certainly, madam. Do you have a receipt?"

"Yes, of course." Emily pulled it out of her bag and handed it to him.

He read it carefully, then said, "I'm sorry, but this item was purchased on sale. The receipt is clearly stamped Nonreturnable." He shoved it back at her.

"But the statue doesn't suit my living room," Emily persisted.

The man took a deep, pained breath and let it out on a long-suffering sigh. "Madam, I'm sorry, but the store's policy is very clear. Sale items can only be returned if they are found to be defective. And that—" he gestured toward the chrome figurine Emily held clutched in her hand "—is clearly not defective. Now, is it?" he asked in a tone that made Emily want to smack him.

"But I don't like it."

"I'm sorry," he repeated. "I cannot break store policy. If you wish, you can return on Monday when the store manager is here and discuss your living-room decor with him." He picked up a pencil and began to write.

"I see. Thank you for all your help." Her irony sailed right over his head. Stuffing the sculpture back into her bag, she sailed out.

She had almost reached the bank of elevators down the hall when Lucas caught up with her.

"Going my way, good-looking?" Lucas asked in a leer.

A man waiting for an elevator glanced from Emily to Lucas in dumbfounded amazement. When Lucas gave him an inquiring look, the man flushed and moved down to the next elevator.

"Behave yourself, Lucas," Emily hissed. "This is serious business."

"I'll say. Did you know that your left hip is much smaller than your right?"

Emily looked down her nose at him. "It's a hereditary defect," she replied with immense dignity. "Besides, didn't your mother ever tell you it was rude to make personal comments?"

"My mother?" His expression froze into formidable lines. "Hardly!"

"Why?" Emily asked, intensely curious about his reaction.

"Why what?"

"Why do you change in some indefinable way every time your mother is mentioned?"

"Do I?" he hedged.

"You look like the Lord High Executioner must have looked right before he chopped off someone's head," she said bluntly.

Lucas frowned, tempted for a moment to tell Emily about his mother—about her alcoholism, her neglect and the psychological abuse she had subjected him to in her more lucid moments. But as he opened his mouth, an image of Rhoda Jones floated into his mind. Unconsciously his lips lifted in a self-derisive smile. Dear, sensitive Rhoda, the most sought-after girl in his

college class. How he'd loved her. He'd been so sure that
his feelings were reciprocated, he'd told her all about
his mother. To his horrified chagrin, she had gently assured him that while she would always consider him a
friend, she felt it would be best if they stopped seeing
each other. She'd read that men who had been abused
as children made terrible husbands and fathers. The
pain of her rejection had faded within weeks, but it had
been much harder to dismiss her words. They'd lin-
gered in his mind like a festering wound that never quite
healed. He'd known that he was just as capable of
forming a mature, loving relationship as anyone else,
but he also knew that Rhoda's views were widely held,
especially among psychologists. And Emily's best
friend was a psychologist.

No, he couldn't risk telling Emily now. He'd tell her
later, when she knew him better.

"Lucas? What's the matter?"

"Nothing, other than the fact that you have an over-
active imagination."

"Undoubtedly." Emily hid her disappointment. If
Lucas didn't want to confide in her, there was nothing
she could do about it. But why did the mere mention of
his mother produce such an intense reaction? Unless... Could his mother have abused him? That would
certainly explain his reaction. Emily wanted to comfort him, but she didn't know how.

Lucas had regained his equilibrium by the time they
arrived at his apartment. He'd taken the cooler she'd
brought with the ingredients for their dinner out of her
car and followed her into the building, all the while
giving a running commentary on the appearance of her

mismatched hips. By the time they'd reached the lobby, Emily was beginning to wish he had turned out to be a sulker. At least, then, she'd have gotten some peace and quiet.

"Afternoon, Mr. Sheridan. Nice..." The voice of the security guard by the front desk trailed away as he got a good look at Emily. He gulped audibly, gave her a weak smile and finished, "Day, isn't it?"

"Absolutely lovely." Lucas gave Emily a besotted smile that confused the poor man even more.

"Honestly, Lucas Sheridan," Emily said, once the elevator doors had closed on the openmouthed guard, "a person can't take you anywhere."

"I have always believed in finding pleasure where I can. And you, Emily McGregor, are turning out to be a source of immense pleasure." He chuckled. "Even if you are a slightly misshapen one."

Emily frowned, wondering about his exact meaning. He could mean he found her very attractive. But he could also mean she was providing him with a lot of laughs—which was not how she preferred him to think of her.

"Tell me," he continued, "why did just the one hip deflate? Why not the whole suit?"

"Because it's made in compartments. You can blow it up as much as you want."

"Oh?" Lucas stared at her oversize bosom and his eyes took on a wicked gleam. "Now, that has possibilities."

"For mayhem," she retorted. "Behave yourself."

"Sorry." He set the cooler down in front of his door while he fished the key out of his pocket. "I plead extenuating circumstances." His gaze slipped to her hip. "Or, more accurately, deflating ones." He unlocked his front door and motioned her inside.

Emily ignored his crack, with the sinking feeling that her mismatched hips were the stuff of which lifelong jokes were made. "If you don't mind, I think I'll change back into myself before we record the results of our experiment."

"Be my guest. My bedroom is through there. Feel free to use anything you need."

Emily picked up her bag, frowning slightly as the movement sent a wave of perfumed air in her direction. She reached into the bag, recoiling when her fingers made contact with a thick, viscous liquid.

Lucas touched the white substance clinging to her fingers, and Emily felt a surge of heat at the contact.

He sniffed it. "Smells good. What is it?"

"Cleansing cream. I mustn't have tightened the bottle properly when I put it back into the bag after I used it." She looked down into the bag and grimaced in annoyance. "It's all over my clothes."

"No problem. I'll run them through the washer while you're changing."

"That was what I was going to change into."

Lucas frowned. "Why don't you put on a pair of my shorts and a shirt? They won't fit very well, but they'll be more comfortable than that bodysuit."

Emily felt a strange twist in the pit of her stomach at the thought of wearing his clothing—of having something that had been next to his skin against her own.

"Thank you," she tried to say naturally. "I'll change and . . ." She paused as she noticed that finally his furniture had arrived.

"You won't have to sit on the floor. That down-filled sofa is more comfortable than my bed."

Her gaze moved to his lips and then skittered down the length of his lean body. The sofa might be more comfortable than his bed, but it couldn't be more interesting. Or more exciting . . .

"It really is." Lucas misunderstood her preoccupied look. "After you get changed, try bouncing on it a few times. And bring that bodysuit back with you. I want to see how it works."

"Sure." Emily gave him an indulgent smile. Lucas was one of the most inquisitive individuals she'd ever met. He was always looking beneath the surface. But what about people? The unexpected thought sent a chill over her skin. Did he apply that same intense curiosity to the people around him? Might he not try to delve into her own past?

Don't be ridiculous. She pulled her imagination up short. *He doesn't even know that you have a past. He probably just thinks that you are normally very leery of allowing personal relationships to develop.*

Despite her determination to hurry, she paused a moment as she entered his bedroom and caught sight of the king-size bed she'd helped him choose. Here, in the relatively small confines of his bedroom, it appeared even bigger than it had in the store. It dominated the room.

Emily gulped, remembering the feel of that mattress beneath her and the warm pressure of his hard body beside her. Determinedly, she looked away from it and continued on into the bathroom. It was also a relatively small room, more functional than elegant, although the huge fluffy towels in bright primary colors added a cheerful touch to the room's basic-white fixtures.

Lucas certainly had well-defined tastes. She fingered a brilliant scarlet towel as she remembered the couch and the armoire he'd bought. What kind of house would he build? she wondered. She shrugged, telling herself that it wasn't any concern of hers. Her association with him was strictly for the length of their research, although—Emily began to slowly strip off her clothes—there was no real reason why they couldn't remain friends. Automatically, she folded the beige dress and set it on the white vanity top. Granted, she couldn't get involved with a man in any permanent way, but there had been absolutely no sign that Lucas was even considering a meaningful, long-term relationship with her—or anyone else, for that matter. He was thirty-six years old and had enormous financial resources. Surely, if marriage and a family had been his goal, he'd have done something about it by now.

She frowned as she wiggled out of the bodysuit. It wasn't as if he'd been making his fortune in some inaccessible place where eligible females were few and far between. San Francisco was one of the most sophisticated cities in the world. If he hadn't found someone he liked in that pool of women, it was because he hadn't been looking. It was because he didn't want a wife and family.

Perhaps, whatever it was that lay at the root of his relationship with his mother had permanently soured him on the idea of children and family? Maybe he preferred to keep his distance from the intimacy and total commitment marriage demanded? In fact, Emily realized with a surge of excitement, that was the most logical explanation for the way he'd lived his life. And that being the case, there couldn't possibly be any harm in letting their friendship continue to grow.

Emily scrubbed the yellow-tinted makeup off her face as she considered his attitude toward her. He was definitely attracted to her. She was much too experienced not to realize that. But did he treat her any differently than he did any other attractive woman? she wondered. Could he be the type of man who found all women a challenge?

Dressed in Lucas's shorts and yellow knit shirt, Emily grimaced. She looked like a little girl playing dress-up, and she didn't want to. She wanted to emphasize her physical features, and for Lucas to see her at her best.

But no one could look their best all the time, and if Lucas was turned off by her less-than-glamorous appearance, then the time to find out was now. Determinedly she went to give him his cooking lesson.

She found him sprawled on the sofa, his black-stocking feet propped up on the glass coffee table they'd chosen, with a pad of paper in his hand. As he looked up and saw her, Emily noticed the flare of some emotion in his eyes, but it was gone before she could identify it.

"Where's the bodysuit?" he asked.

"I forgot to bring it out. You can inspect it after dinner. What are you doing?"

"I thought we should jot down our impressions while they're still fresh. Have a seat." He patted the cushion beside him.

Emily sat down on the sofa about a foot away from him. She forced down a sudden urge to scoot closer—to find out if the muscles of his thighs felt as hard as they looked, to find out if . . .

"Impressions?" The last word of his question penetrated her fantasy and Emily blinked, staring at him blankly.

Lucas frowned and pressed the back of his hand against her cheek.

Emily's eyes widened at the shivery sensation that shot through her as his knuckles brushed across her skin.

"Are you okay?" Lucas demanded. "Did that bodysuit raise your temperature and make you spacey?"

"No. I'm normally this spacey," she said dryly. "Now, quit playing doctor and get on with it."

"Spoilsport." His eyes danced with laughter. "Playing doctor with you sounds like every man's fantasy."

"Yeah, but what do I get out of it?"

"Well . . ." He tilted his head to one side and studied her. Then, with seeming casualness, he reached out and slipped his hand beneath her soft curls, grasping the back of her neck.

Emily looked at him uncertainly, mistrusting the wolfish glint in his eyes. The green in them seemed to have intensified. He tugged, pulling her toward him with a steady force that didn't threaten, but wouldn't be denied. Nervously, Emily licked her dry lips. "What are you doing?"

"I presume that's a rhetorical question?" he murmured against her mouth.

The warmth of his breath wafted across her face, causing the skin on her cheeks to tighten.

"I don't..." Her halfhearted objection was swallowed up as his mouth closed over hers. Its firm pressure molded her lips to his, and with a sigh, she relaxed into him. Her breasts brushed against the hard wall of his chest, swelling under the impact. Instinctively Emily pressed closer, and her nipples contracted with almost-painful intensity.

Lucas's arms tightened encouragingly, and he traced over her lower lip with the tip of his tongue.

Longingly, she opened her mouth and his tongue surged inside. The taste of him seemed to flood her senses, and she trembled.

To her intense disappointment Lucas lifted his head, leaving her feeling bereft. Emily opened eyes that seemed glued together and stared up at him. His features were taut, sharpened by desire. A surge of intense exhilaration filled her that their kiss could have moved him so; but the very strength of that exhilaration made Emily decide to cool things off.

She scooted back against the sofa arm and reminded, "You were saying something about getting our thoughts down."

He gave her a rueful grin. "At this moment, my thoughts would burn a hole through the paper."

"Umm, yes," Emily murmured, feeling shy. "Now, about our research. What did you see?"

"I found our would-be Lothario rather interesting. Particularly his body language."

Emily frowned. "Body language? You mean like the fact that while I was in my disguise he never really looked at me? There was no eye contact like the first time."

Lucas snorted, "Eye contact! Hell, he was practically devouring you with his eyes. I was waiting for him to grab you."

"Yes," Emily agreed. "Our Mr. Lane did seem to be operating on sensual overload. I doubt he really paid much attention to what I was actually saying. He simply wanted to score points."

Lucas frowned thoughtfully. "What still astounds me is that he saw no connection with you in the disguise. He wasn't even suspicious."

"I told you," Emily said patiently, "he never really looked. He categorized me as unattractive, and gave me the absolute minimum of attention he could get away with."

"You know," Lucas remarked, "Marcy is doing this from a woman's perspective, but there are some significant business ramifications here."

Emily looked uncomprehending. "How so?"

"How did you feel when he brushed you off like yesterday's news?"

Emily thought back. "Faintly amused at his lack of perception and annoyed at his brusque manner. I think I'd be angry if I met with that dismissive attitude very often."

"Precisely. You wouldn't feel like spending much money in that store, would you?"

"No," she admitted.

"So, a retail business that wanted to sell more would need to train its personnel to consider all its customers beautiful. We'll have to ask Marcy if she intends to explore that aspect of the research."

Why? Emily wondered. *Because you really want to know, or because it's a good excuse to talk to her?*

"I'll see her tomorrow," Emily offered, as a way of finding out.

"Good. Then you can ask her. But enough of Marcy. I'm starving. Let's begin our cooking lesson."

Emily gave him a brilliant smile, refusing to admit, even to herself, her relief at his casual dismissal of Marcy. "You're on. I'll teach. You cook."

7

LUCAS ACCEPTED the plastic bag of cubed, raw chicken she handed him, squinted doubtfully at it and then asked, "What exactly did you say we were making for dinner?"

"A fruited chicken dish for the main course, a lettuce-and-tomato salad and scones." She finished pulling out the containers.

"Scones?" He studied the plastic bowl of flour mixture she was opening. "You mean like they cook on a griddle in Scotland?"

"No, I mean like they cook in the oven in America. You do have eggs and milk, don't you?"

"Of course." He beamed at her. "I went to the grocery store."

Emily opened the refrigerator and jumped back as something fell out and landed on the floor at her feet. "It looks like you brought a goodly portion of the store home with you."

She picked up the package and read the label. "Anchovy paste? Good Lord, it's true."

"What's true?" He took the tube from her and shoved it back into the already overcrowded bottom shelf before digging out the milk and eggs.

"My mother says that she doesn't dare turn my father loose in a grocery store because men will invariably come home with the most improbable things. I always thought she was joking, but it's true."

"It is not. Anchovy paste has lots of uses."

"Such as? I've never encountered a recipe that used it before."

"Well," he began and then stopped as he realized that he could hardly tell her what kind of recipes called for anchovy paste without also revealing just how extensive his knowledge of cooking was. Frustrated, he finally demanded, "What have you got against anchovy paste?"

"Nothing. It's just not the kind of thing I expect to find in a refrigerator. Do you happen to have a decent-size mixing bowl?"

Lucas set one on the counter. "Of all the parochial attitudes—"

"This is the Midwest, my friend. It's full of parochial attitudes—or hadn't you noticed?"

"Every place is full of parochial attitudes. It's just that what's parochial changes from place to place."

Emily stopped greasing the disposable cookie sheet she'd brought as she considered his words. "You could well have a point. I'll have to mention it to Marcy. It sounds like it's right up her alley."

"I wouldn't if I were you or we'll be liable to find ourselves drafted for another study."

"True. Marcy has always had a nasty habit of embroiling her friends in her latest enthusiasm."

"Thank God, I'm not one of them," he replied with obvious relief.

Emily laughed. "I hate to disappoint you, but everyone is Marcy's friend when she's looking for victims. Now, then, wash your hands and we'll get started."

"Yes, *Nanny.*" Despite his mocking tone, he obediently picked up a bar of soap beside the sink and began to meticulously work up a lather.

Emily watched as the soap squeezed out from between his long fingers. The translucent bubbles gleamed against his tanned skin. She remembered the strength of those fingers as they'd held her against him.

"What do I get to do?"

"You get to cook. I'm a great believer in hands-on experience."

"Oh?" There was that teasing light in his eyes again.

"And in maintaining the proper distance between a student and the teacher," she added for good measure.

"Oh, I am, too." The gleam in his eye intensified and Emily instinctively retreated, only to find her back pressed up against the counter.

"But the question, dear teacher, is what is the proper distance? Precision is so important in communication, don't you think? Now, this is not the proper distance between us. You're too far away. It's off-putting," he complained.

"I'd like to put you off," Emily muttered as he moved closer still, stopping a scant inch from her.

"No, this isn't the proper distance, either," he decided. "This close I can smell the perfume you're wearing, and I find it somewhat distracting."

He found being this close *somewhat* distracting! She was so distracted she was finding it difficult to remember what it was they were supposed to be doing.

"On the other hand," he continued.

"That's three hands and it was two too many." She put her hands on his chest, intending to push him away, but when she touched him, his body heat seemed to glue her fingers to him. She could feel the springy texture of his chest hair beneath the thin material of his knit shirt. It tickled her palms, sending waves of longing radiating through her. Determinedly, she fought the urge to explore the sensation and pushed against him.

He didn't budge.

"Is this another experiment of some sort?" He gave her an impossibly innocent grin.

"No, it's a prelude to mayhem. We're supposed to be cooking."

"We are. We are," he agreed enthusiastically. "And I can hardly wait to see what develops."

Emily smiled at him reluctantly. "Lucas Sheridan, you're incorrigible."

"No, Emily McGregor." He cupped her chin in his hand and tilted her head back. "What I am is a man, and what you are is a very intriguing woman full of infinite promise."

Lucas watched with a sense of helpless frustration as her eyes darkened and her mouth compressed with pain. What was the matter? Why had she so suddenly and completely withdrawn from the teasing nonsense they'd been sharing? If he didn't find out what was bothering her and find out soon, it was going to drive him mad. He'd only known her for a short time, and already she consumed his thoughts to a degree that he found vaguely alarming. All he could think about was the feel and the taste of her mouth beneath his; of what it would be like to make love to her.

He took a deep breath, knowing that he needed to back off and give her a little breathing space, even if he didn't know why.

He turned to survey the ingredients on the counter. "What should I do first?"

Gratefully, Emily followed his lead. "Break an egg into the bowl and beat it up a little with a fork."

"Check." He deliberately smacked the egg on the edge of the bowl, shattering the shell and sending the yolk oozing half in and half out of the bowl. He studied the resultant mess for a few seconds and then asked, "How does one get the eggshells out?"

"By not getting them in in the first place," she said with resignation.

"The time to tell me that was before I broke the egg." His premeditated disaster erased the tension from her face.

"Dump the whole mess down the garbage disposal, wipe out the bowl with a paper towel and try again," she instructed.

Once he'd done that, Emily handed him a second egg and watched as he carefully cracked it on the edge of the counter before opening it over the bowl. He gave her a triumphant grin of achievement that flashed a curious warmth through her.

"Now beat it with a fork," she ordered. While he did that, she opened a small can of evaporated milk and handed it to him. "Add that and then the flour mixture."

She leaned her elbows on the counter and rested her chin on the palm of her hand, watching in fascination as the muscles in his arms rippled while he stirred the heavy mixture.

"All mixed," he said in satisfaction.

"Very good," she praised, and his smile widened. "Now—" she sprinkled a liberal amount of flour on the counter "—put your dough on that."

Emily coughed as he promptly upended the bowl on the counter, sending flour flying in all directions. She waved a hand to clear the air. "You're going to knead it," she told him.

"I know I need it, but what do I do with it?"

"No, not need as in want. Knead as in to gently push and pound. Here, I'll show you," she offered when he continued to stare blankly at her.

She dusted her hands with flour and pressed the heels of her palms into the dough. To her surprise, Lucas stepped behind her and, reaching around her, placed his hands over hers.

"Now, how do we knead?"

She could feel him in every cell of her body, and the sensation was playing havoc with her coordination. "Like—" she steadied her voice "—like this." She pushed down on the dough and his palms pressed into the backs of her hands. The pressure transmitted a shower of tiny explosions of pleasure that, no matter how much she tried to tell herself were inappropriate to the situation, she couldn't entirely banish. Emily took a deep breath and then wished she hadn't when it forced her even closer to him. Since she didn't seem to be able to avoid his closeness, she decided that the next best thing to do would be to get the kneading over with as quickly as possible.

She put the dough through a very hasty process and then stepped outside the circle of his arms, ignoring the feeling of depravation that engulfed her.

"Shape the dough into an eight-inch circle and put it on the cookie sheet," she directed him. "While it's baking, we can fix the main course." *With you working on one side of the counter and me on the other,* she decided.

Once the scones were in the oven, Emily handed Lucas the sack of fruit and told him to cut them into equal-size pieces. She ignored him as she browned the cubed chicken and made the orange sauce.

"I'm all done with the fruit," Lucas announced and peered over her shoulder at the mixture she was stirring.

"Then arrange the chicken around the edge of that plate and microwave it at full power for four minutes."

After washing the utensils they'd used, she was eyeing the flour-covered counter where he'd so enthusiastically kneaded the scones when a hiss followed by an angry pop came from the microwave. She walked over to it, followed by the more cautious Lucas.

"What's the matter with that thing?" Lucas peered through the glass door from behind her.

"Considering that you're the one who put the chicken in there, the possibilities are endless," she replied.

"A basic tenet of good management is to work toward the solution of a problem. Not to spend your time assigning the blame for it," Lucas said virtuously.

"Can you be managed?" Emily's eyes gleamed with laughter.

"You can lead a horse to water, but you can't make him drink."

"I wonder if I could manage to shut off your supply of bromides. You—" She jumped as something popped in the microwave again.

Curious, she opened the door just in time to be hit by bits of flying grape.

"Close that door! We're under attack." Lucas reached around her and slammed the door shut.

"Where's the plastic wrap?" she demanded.

"In the drawer." He brushed away a bit of grape that clung to the front of her shirt. Emily felt a jolt of desire shaft through her as his fingers brushed up against the side of her breast.

She swallowed and forced her mind back to the problem of the flying fruit. "Why isn't it on the chicken?"

Lucas cocked his head to one side and stared at her in puzzlement. "Is your question a non sequitur?" he finally asked.

"No, it's a perfectly reasonable question." She made a valiant effort to focus on plastic wrap when what really interested her was Lucas. It was a task that became almost impossible when he began to carefully remove each and every bit of grape.

"You're supposed to put the plastic wrap over the chicken dish."

"You didn't tell me to," he explained, "and how was I supposed to know if you don't tell me? You're the teacher."

No. You're the one teaching me the finer points of frustration! Emily trembled as the back of his hand swept over the tip of her breast. She took a deep breath, but to her dismay, the movement revealed her body's reaction to him. Her nipples had hardened into tight buds. Furtively, she hunched her shoulders forward, hoping to hide the fact.

"Hold still," Lucas ordered.

"What are you doing?" She grabbed his hand, which was hovering around her left breast.

"Trying to get rid of the grape pieces, of course."

"Leave them alone," she said. "I don't mind."

"I do. That's one of my favorite shirts you're wearing. Not that it doesn't look a whole lot better on you than it ever did on me." His gaze dropped to her chest, then a faint red flush stained his cheeks.

"In fact—" his voice dropped to a husky whisper, setting her nerves jangling "—there's no contest at all."

His fingers traced over her left eyebrow and down her jawline. "Did you know that your skin feels like velvet—soft and smooth and infinitely desirable?"

Emily nervously licked her lips, as her gaze was caught and held by the desire she saw smoldering in his eyes.

His wandering forefinger continued its tracing over her lips, and she shuddered. Her breathing quickened and she parted her lips slightly. His finger followed, moving over her bottom lip and flooding her mouth with the taste of salt.

He leaned back, bracing himself against the counter, and pulled her between his legs. "You're so beautiful."

He slipped his hands beneath the oversize shirt and pulled her closer to him.

Emily burned at the feel of his hard thighs and the strength of the hand he held splayed across her bare back. There was an insistent throbbing in her pelvic area that was fast drowning out all rational thought.

"So very beautiful." His breath wafted over her cheek, making the skin tighten. "So absolutely beautiful," he crooned against her mouth. The tip of his tongue lightly stroked over her bottom lip, sending a curl of anticipation through her.

Holding her pressed firmly against him with one hand, he slipped his other hand beneath her shirt to find and cup her bare breast.

Emily gasped at the torrent of sensations that shook her and she looked into his eyes and was startled by the ardor she saw there.

"So very beautiful . . ." He repeated the litany soothingly, but she didn't find it soothing at all. She felt as if she'd die if he didn't kiss her.

As if reading her desire, he lowered his head a fraction and pressed his lips to hers. Emily's parted eagerly to allow his probing tongue entry, and the strangest feeling surged through her—as if she'd just discovered something infinitely precious. And she pressed against his hand, reveling in the feel of his roughened palm brushing over her sensitive breast. But before she had a chance to properly explore it, Lucas lifted his head.

"The timer for the scones went off. It we don't take the damn things out, they'll burn."

Emily made a valiant effort to regain control of her rioting senses. Later, she'd examine her unprecedented reaction to Lucas's kiss. Right now, she was going to share what was left of their dinner with him and make normal conversation like the competent woman she knew herself to be.

DESPITE WORRYING THE problem of her growing attraction to Lucas around in her mind for the rest of the week, she still hadn't reached any conclusions about her susceptibility to Lucas when Marcy appeared the following Wednesday afternoon.

Marcy frowned when she caught sight of Emily's pale features. "What's wrong? You look—"

"Hi, Marcy."

"Don't try to change the subject!"

Emily smiled. "And here I thought I was merely observing the social amenities. I should have better sense than to try a normal response on a psychologist. And, speaking of knowing better, where did you buy that awful puce—" Emily waved her hand in the air as if reaching for the right word "—thing you're wearing?"

"Dress!" Marcy said indignantly. "It's the latest fashion. Don't you like it?"

"On you, no!" Emily responded with the bluntness of long-standing friendship. "That color makes your complexion look muddy, and all that material hides your figure."

"That was the idea," Marcy explained. "But forget my love handles and tell me why you looked so . . . so triste."

"Nauseated would be closer to the mark, and it's because of this." She gestured with the paper she'd been reading. "It's a grad student's proposed doctoral dissertation."

"What's it about?" Marcy extracted a soda from Emily's tiny refrigerator, opened it, took a long swallow and then sighed happily.

"The various and sundry tortures used during the French and Indian War."

Marcy blinked at Emily. "Tortures as in painful?"

Emily grimaced. "In graphic detail. And, speaking of pain, what do you know about the adult children of abusive mothers?"

Marcy sighed. "More than I wish I did. Child abuse is still a lot more prevalent in our society than many people realize or care to admit. Why? Have you run across it?"

"Not exactly." Emily scrambled for a way to ask her question without letting Marcy know what she suspected about Lucas's childhood. "What I want to know is how having had an abusive mother affects the child when he or she grows up?" she finally asked.

"In what regard?"

"In forming adult relationships. For example, would an abused child want to have a spouse and/or children?"

Marcy shrugged. "It depends. They could rush into marriage at a young age and have a family out of a desire to do it right, so to speak. Or they could go to the opposite extreme and never marry, having been soured on the idea of a close personal relationship. In order to be more specific, I'd need more facts. Everything I'm telling you is just conjecture."

"So's life." Emily decided she'd said enough. She didn't want Marcy to guess that she was talking about Lucas. And she most emphatically didn't want Marcy suspecting to what extent Lucas was dominating her thoughts.

"And speaking of conjecture—" Emily moved on to divert Marcy "—Lucas and I started working on your study last Saturday by attempting to return a sale item at Winthrops."

"What did you conclude?" Marcy asked eagerly.

"That the toilet stalls in the ladies' room are too small."

"What?" Marcy looked puzzled.

"Never mind. It's a long story. But it went about like we'd expected. I batted my eyelashes at the clerk and he fell all over himself to break the rules for me."

Marcy sighed. "Men can be remarkably obtuse when they run up against a beautiful woman."

"So can women," Emily added grimly. "An amazing number take one look at me, decide I'm going to snaffle their boyfriends, and avoid me like the plague."

"Maybe. But the reason I introduced myself to you all those years ago at that grad-school reception was because of the way the men were congregated around you."

Emily frowned. "I don't follow."

"Simple logic. You couldn't possibly date all the men who fancied you, so I figured I could have my choice of the leftovers."

"And all these years I've thought it was my sparkling personality. I should have known there was a more devious reason. Tell me, if your goal was to find a man, why haven't you married one?"

"I've been tempted a few times, but I keep thinking about what would happen if I married someone and then met someone else who appealed to me more. I'd be stuck."

"But what about falling in love?" Emily asked.

"Oh, I do that all the time," Marcy assured her. "I just can't seem to stay in love. After about a week, the rosy glow begins to fade, and I start to notice things." She grimaced. "Believe me, it's fatal to look too closely at a man, especially one you're emotionally involved with."

"That was one of the things we noticed about the clerk."

"What?"

"He never really looked at me when I was unattractive. His glance kind of skidded off me as if I weren't actually there."

"That's interesting. Was he rude?"

"No, not really," Emily said slowly. "His were the sins of omission, not commission. He gave me the absolute minimum of attention and manners he could get away with. He treated me as if I were a necessary evil that he wanted to get over with as quickly as possible. Lucas thinks that this study of yours could have implications for sales training courses."

"Hmm." Marcy rubbed the tip of her nose thoughtfully. "I wonder how fashionable clothes worn by an uglified woman would have affected the clerk's reaction."

"I don't know. He seemed to be reacting to me as an unappetizing package, as opposed to a collection of parts."

"Speaking of a collection of fascinating parts, how's Lucas?"

"Fascinating," Emily said.

"You find him fascinating?" Marcy persisted.

"Of course, I find him fascinating. I'm sterile, not dead."

"You're damn pigheaded," Marcy snapped. "Would you forget that!"

. Emily sighed. "I wish I could."

"But—" Marcy paused as the phone rang.

"Emily, this is Lucas," he said unnecessarily when she answered the phone. She'd know his voice anywhere. "Are you busy?"

"Why?" she asked cautiously.

"Because I need your help with a teaching problem. Could you get over to my office as soon as possible?"

Emily looked at Marcy, weighed talking to her against seeing Lucas, and instantly consigned Marcy to oblivion.

"I'll be there in five minutes."

"Don't knock, just walk in. And, Emily—" he paused as if choosing his words "—please go along with what I say."

"But what—" She realized he'd broken the connection. What kind of problem did he have? She hung up the phone. Knowing Lucas, the possibilities were endless.

"That was Lucas, and he wants me." Emily got to her feet. "I think I'm to be the cavalry."

"This I've got to see."

Emily grinned at her. "You weren't invited. Go away."

"All right. But I want a full report later." Marcy gave in gracefully.

8

EMILY PAUSED AS SHE read Lucas's name engraved on the brass plate of the door in front of her. Her heartbeat accelerated as she reached out and traced over the lettering. The chill of the metal penetrated her skin, jarring her out of her absorption. She shook her head and walked in.

Emily gaped in surprise as she took in the scene in front of her. Lucas was seated in a black leather swivel chair behind a huge mahogany desk. Perched on the edge of that desk, not two feet from him, was a gorgeous blonde who was pointing toward something on the computer printout sheet she was showing him.

As the woman looked up, startled by Emily's unannounced entrance, Emily caught the diamondlike sparkle of tears in her long eyelashes. Her long *fake* eyelashes, Emily observed with a flash of jealousy, the intensity of which startled her.

"I beg your pardon, but I was talking to Mr. Sheridan." The blonde's brilliant green eyes flashed with annoyance.

Tinted contacts. She summoned up her best mature-adult-to-fractious-child smile—a smile that over the years of teaching she'd developed into an art form—and said, "You don't have to apologize. It's all right."

"Darling—" Lucas's blatantly sensual tone sparked a jolt of response in Emily "—you managed to get out of your meeting early. Now we'll have more time for ourselves." His voice deepened suggestively, and Emily caught her breath at the images that sprang into her mind.

"Wait till you see what I bought us this morning," he added.

"Animal, vegetable or mineral?" she asked, totally unable to resist him in this mood.

He chuckled. "You'll just have to wait until we're alone to find out. In the meantime, I'd like you to meet one of my students, Jessica Wood. Jessica, this is Dr. McGregor."

Emily nodded at the young woman who'd been watching the byplay with barely concealed chagrin and then asked Lucas, "How long is this treat to be delayed?"

He smiled indulgently. "Not long. I told Miss Wood when she asked to speak to me that I couldn't give her much information on course selection in the accounting department."

Course selection, nothing! Man selection more likely, Emily thought cynically.

"Perhaps I should come back at a more convenient time?" The young woman gave Emily a frustrated look.

"There's really no need, Miss Wood," Lucas said gently. "I think I've given you as much help as I can."

He shrugged, and Emily watched as his powerful shoulders moved underneath his crisp white shirt. Her mouth dried as she remembered the feel of those shoulders beneath her fingers.

"But I'm still not quite sure . . ." Miss Wood continued doggedly.

"Then I suggest that you ask one of the professors in the accounting department."

Emily had no trouble recognizing the impatience behind his words. To her surprise, Miss Wood seemed totally unaware of his feelings.

"That won't be necessary." The blonde gave him a bravely appealing look. "I'll try what you've suggested and see how it works."

"You do that." Lucas's smile was dismissive.

"It was nice meeting you, Miss Wood," Emily lied as she held the door open for the young woman.

"Same here," Miss Wood muttered as, with one last frustrated glance at Lucas's impassive face, she left.

Emily closed the door behind her and leaned back against it. She frowned as she studied Lucas.

"Am I to be told the verdict?" he finally asked.

"I like your tie—did you know that it's the Sixteenth Queen's Royal Lancers' regimental stripe? And, what part was I playing in that little drama?"

"Thanks. I didn't know, but it's not surprising since I bought it in England. And it wasn't a drama—it was a farce."

"I still want to know what role I was playing." She left the protection of the door and walked over to his desk.

"Well . . ." To her amazement, he seemed embarrassed. His cheekbones were flushed a dull red and he tugged on his earlobe. "Miss Wood is—" He gestured ineffectually.

"Has you firmly in her sights?" Emily prompted.

"Something like that. I think I was slated to be her next conquest. She's in one of my classes, and she's made an excuse to stop and talk to me after every session. When she called earlier and asked if she could come over and discuss her schedule . . ." He grimaced. "It didn't take a genius to figure out what she had on her mind. So I called you."

"Why?" Emily ignored the pleasure she felt at his admission in favor of finding out a few facts.

"Why! I should think it's obvious. No man who had his choice between a beautiful, mature woman like you and a pretty kid like her could possibly want her. I was hoping that she'd get the message without my having to come right out and say so. That way her pride would still be intact and, hopefully, we could still function in a teacher-pupil relationship."

Emily perched on the cleared space on his desk where Miss Wood had been sitting. "I think you're being overly optimistic," she finally said. "I doubt she'll give up quite that easily. She seemed more annoyed with me than with you. And one thing I've noticed is that people who want something are capable of enormous self-deception in the pursuit of that goal."

He grimaced. "I certainly hope not."

"You know—" she eyed him thoughtfully "—I never considered sexual harassment from the male point of view. Do you often get cornered behind your desk by predatory females?"

"Not out in the real world. The women I worked with were mature enough to convey their interest in a way that allowed me to respond or not without either party losing face. Miss Wood is too young to have learned the technique."

He leaned back in his chair and studied her. "Now you, on the other hand, are a master at freezing out a man's interest." He'd decided to risk probing behind her initial withdrawal from him. To his annoyance, she sidestepped the implied question.

"I thought men liked younger women."

"I can't say anything about men in general but, personally, I like a woman I can talk to. And she has to have lived long enough and done enough and know enough to be able to carry on a conversation."

"But Miss Wood is gorgeous," Emily persisted, not sure why she didn't just let the subject drop.

"True." His prompt agreement hurt. "But her looks are more a promise of what she might become in a few years. You know, Emily, I've often thought that it's only the very young or the very immature who form relationships based on physical appearance. One might be attracted to beauty, but beauty by itself isn't enough to hold one's interest."

Emily felt a tiny glow of warmth at his words before she remembered that the reason he was seeing her was Marcy's study. But then again, he was beginning to find her as fascinating as she found him. She'd stake her last dollar that he had found the kisses they'd shared exciting. There was no way he could have faked his body's reaction to her.

"What are you thinking about, Emily?" Lucas asked softly.

"About kissing you. I was remembering how it felt. How you felt."

"And?" he prodded.

"I'd like to do it again," she admitted.

"Please do," he invited. "You aren't the only one who remembers."

Emily scooted closer until she was sitting directly in front of him. The smoothly polished fabric of his pants brushed against her nylon-clad leg, sending a tremor of awareness through her. Enjoying the unexpected sensation of being the one totally in control, she leaned forward and began to explore his jaw with her fingertips. The faintly abrasive texture of his emerging beard scraped across her sensitive skin, raising goose bumps on her arm.

"You have a very heavy beard," she remarked, continuing her exploration of the texture and shape of his chin.

"Uh-huh." His voice deepened. "I'll have to shave again this evening."

Emily ignored the implications of that in favor of concentrating on her tactile exploration. She ran her finger down the bridge of his nose, frowning when she discovered a very slight bump beneath the smooth surface of his skin.

"I was hit in the face with a hockey stick when I was in high school," he answered her unspoken question.

Emily moved on, her fingers seeking out his lips. They were surprisingly soft to her touch, and she shifted restlessly as she remembered the feel of them against her mouth. Remembered the damp heat of his breath as it warmed her skin.

Lucas reached out and gently tugged her forward, tumbling her into his lap. Emily snuggled closer, reveling in the feel of his hard thighs beneath her soft hips. The gorgeous blonde had left him cold, but she turned him on merely by touching him. The knowledge bubbled through her like vintage champagne.

"Emily, I think—"

"This has nothing to do with thinking," she whispered as her fingers worried a button on his shirt free. She pushed her hand inside, and her palm caught in the crisp hair on his chest.

"You're right," he agreed. "This definitely comes under the heading of Instinctive Behavior." His mouth covered hers with rough hunger.

Eagerly, Emily pressed closer to him. She wanted this with a need that would have appalled her if she'd been rational enough to appreciate its depth.

"Oh! I'm so sorry!" A shrill voice poured over Emily's heated senses like a cascade of icy water. Lucas lifted his head and she started to turn hers, but Lucas's fingers gently forced her flushed features against the crisp white cotton of his shirt.

"I did knock, but no one answered. I forgot to take my notebook when I left," the voice babbled.

Miss Wood. Emily surfaced enough to put a name to it.

"The next time you knock on a door and don't receive an answer, I suggest you leave," Lucas retorted, making no attempt whatsoever to soften the anger coloring his voice.

"I'm so sorry! I didn't mean—" Miss Wood stammered. She hastily scooped up her notepad and left.

Lucas glared at the closed door for a second and then glanced down at Emily, his features softening miraculously. "Now, where were we?"

Escaping the real world, she thought grimly, wondering what it was about this man that made her forget everything but the necessity of getting close to him. And in some inexplicable way he was becoming necessary to her, and that unpalatable fact sent a chill of reality through her. She needed to step back and think about what she was doing.

Determinedly she scooted off his lap, ignoring his disappointed expression.

"You know, Lucas, I'll give you odds that she came back deliberately."

He frowned. "Why would she do that?"

"To check out the competition, of course. I think she wanted to see just how deeply involved we were. And now that I've done my good deed for the day, I'd better be off."

"You can't go yet." He got to his feet. "You haven't seen what I bought this morning." He took a large brown paper sack off the top of his filing cabinet.

Emily watched as he pulled a medium-size metal pot out of the sack.

"See!" He held it up triumphantly. "We're going to use this to cook dinner this evening."

She finally recognized what it was. "That's a pressure cooker. Where'd you get it?"

"I passed a garage sale this morning, and I stopped. They had the most fascinating collection of stuff," he enthused. "I thought we could use this to make beef stew for dinner. I've got all the ingredients at home."

Emily studied the pot uncertainly. "I've never used a pressure cooker before. Did it come with instructions?"

"No, but the lady who sold it to me explained how it worked. Are you game to give it a try?"

"I'll try anything once," she said, responding more to the gleam in his eye than to any desire to fiddle with a pressure cooker.

"Now, that's a philosophy that deserves further exploration. Let's get out of here before Miss Wood decides to have another go at capturing my bank account."

Emily eyed him thoughtfully and then said, "No, I don't think so."

"You think we've finally scared her off?"

"Who knows, but that wasn't what I was referring to. I don't think your bank account is your primary attraction."

"No doubt she fell for my handsome face," he scoffed. "She sure wasn't attracted to my personality, because she doesn't know the first thing about me."

"She knows that you were kind enough not to be brutally frank or unscrupulous enough to become involved with a student. And I'll grant that you aren't handsome in the classic sense of the word, but then men like you don't need to be."

"We don't?"

"No, you don't," she replied. "Remember, I once told you that to a woman the most powerful aphrodisiac going is power. As a rich businessman, power is a commodity you have a lot of."

"I sold the business," he reminded her.

"But you didn't sell the attitude of being the boss," she struggled to explain. "It permeates your whole personality. I have the feeling that you're going to be beating off young women at the start of every semester for as long as you teach."

Lucas frowned. "Do you have this problem?"

"Nope. I've never had a young woman proposition me."

"I'm serious, Emily."

"I usually get one or two young men a year who wallow in an excess of hormones every time they see me."

"So, how do you handle it?"

"As a short-term nuisance that, if ignored, will go away. It almost always does."

"Hmm. I'll have to think about that, but at the moment I'm starving and I want to try out my pressure cooker. Come on." He handed her the pot, picked up his bulging briefcase and opened the door. He cast a furtive look down the hallway and announced, "The coast is clear. Let's make our escape."

By the time Emily had helped Lucas prepare the vegetables for the stew, she was the one contemplating escape. Her nerves were frayed and her level of frustration was skyrocketing. It seemed to her as if Lucas was constantly brushing up against her. The only thing that made it bearable was that she was relatively certain it was unintentional on his part. In a kitchen as small as his, it was no wonder he kept brushing up against her. The wonder was that he hadn't tripped over her. Surreptitiously, she watched with amused tenderness as he meticulously cut the beef into cubes.

"There." Lucas set down the lethal-looking knife he'd been welding. "That ought to do it. Hand me the pressure cooker, would you?"

Emily gave it to him and then climbed up on one of the breakfast barstools to watch as he carefully layered the meat and vegetables. He frowned slightly as he studied the finished results.

Emily craned her neck and looked in. Everything seemed fine to her. At least as fine as it could be, given that she didn't really know what they were supposed to be doing.

"What's wrong?" she finally asked.

"This needs a rutabaga."

"*Nothing* needs a rutabaga," she said emphatically. "Why don't you throw in a few spices instead?"

"Good idea." He liberally sprinkled some pepper on top.

"How about some thyme?" she suggested when he made no move to add anything else.

He glanced up. "You can have all the time you want."

"And all the bad jokes, too," she countered wryly. "Don't you have anything a little more adventurous than pepper?"

"You've got something against pepper?"

"No, but by itself it's rather bland. It needs sprucing up."

"That's what the rutabaga was for," he mourned.

Emily gave up. Lucas's taste buds definitely needed to be educated.

She watched as he fiddled with a device on the lid before he sealed the pot.

"You know," she remarked slowly, "I don't think I've ever seen anyone use a pressure cooker before."

"My father used to use one quite a bit when he got home from work and wanted to fix supper in a hurry."

"Your mother and father were divorced then?" Emily tried to make the question sound casual. She watched as his face set in the now familiar hard lines that any mention of his mother seemed to precipitate.

Lucas stared into Emily's eyes, seeing only concern mirrored there. *Tell her*, he prodded himself. *She has to know sometime. So tell her. But how?* How could he gently slip it in without making it seem as if he himself placed undue importance on his miserable childhood.

"I didn't mean to pry," Emily apologized, trying to retrieve the situation when he continued to stare at her.

"You aren't prying. I was just..." He took a deep breath and blurted out, "My father did the cooking because my mother was usually dead drunk by that time of day, which was a blessing in disguise because when she was sober, her aim was better." Fatalistically, Lucas braced himself for her response.

"Your mother is to be pitied," Emily responded thoughtfully.

"Pitied!" he exclaimed in shock. "The one who should be pitied is my poor father. He worked himself into an early grave with two jobs and all the housework. And for what? A drunken bitch of a woman who never had a decent impulse in her life." Lucas gave the lid of the pressure cooker a vicious twist.

Emily bit her lip, uncertain what to do. Part of her wanted to just drop the subject, but she was hesitant to do that. This was the first time Lucas had opened up.

She knew how hard he must have found it. If she simply changed the subject, Lucas might think that his feelings were of no importance to her. While she knew that a few words from her weren't going to cure a lifetime of bitter memories, she might be able to start him thinking along different lines.

Emily took a deep breath and let it out slowly. "Yes, your father deserves your sympathy, but he also has to share some of the censure."

"Censure!"

Emily leaned toward him, willing him to listen, to really listen to what she was saying. "Lucas, I don't pretend to be an expert, but I am well-read. And I know that alcoholics don't drink in a vacuum. Your father made it possible for your mother to drink like that. Without his paying the bills, buying the liquor and cleaning up after her, she would have found it much more difficult to be a drunk."

"She'd still have done it," Lucas insisted.

"Probably," Emily admitted. "But your father was not an innocent victim. He stayed in that relationship for his own reasons. The only innocent victim was you."

Lucas felt confused by Emily's unexpected interpretation of what he had told her. He knew his mother was the one at fault. Why couldn't Emily see that? But as long as what he'd revealed hadn't changed how she viewed him, did he really care whom she blamed? This was clearly a case of quitting while he was ahead.

"Forget it, Emily." He made an almost-visible effort to subdue his emotions. "I'm not sure how we got on such a depressing subject, anyway."

"It was all the rutabaga's fault," she quipped, realizing that she'd said enough for the moment. Probably more than enough. One thing she did know was that he was never going to be really free of the past until he'd learned to forgive his mother.

"Maybe we should stick to turnips." He set the pressure cooker on the stove and turned on the burner.

"You're too late. I already read the Little House books."

He stared at her, curiosity replacing the emotional turmoil in his eyes. "I know I'm going to be sorry I asked, but what does a book have to do with turnips in the stew?"

"I read the series when I was about eight, and one of the little girls in it loved to eat raw turnips. So I pestered my mother until she bought me one." Emily shuddered at the memory.

"Be grateful you never read *Fried Worms*."

Emily stared at him in horror. "Fried what?"

"Worms. It really is a book. I was with a friend of mine when he bought it for his kid."

"Yuck! I may have been impetuous, but I wasn't stupid."

"No, I'll bet you were a very clever little girl. Clever, with Shirley Temple curls and frilly dresses covered with yards of lace and ruffles."

Emily snorted. "I was terminally shy, with long black braids, jeans and braces. And when the braces came off, the acne came out. However, I was smart. Very smart," she finished smugly.

He laughed. "I'll bet you were also incorrigible. Come on. Enough about the past." He threw his arm around her shoulder. "Let's go plan the future. What are we doing next for Marcy's study?"

Emily momentarily allowed herself to savor the feel of his strength as they walked into his living room. Once there, however, she made a determined effort to keep her distance, telling herself that they were there to work on Marcy's project, not to indulge her growing physical fascination with Lucas.

Lucas watched in disappointment as she sank down onto one of the cream chairs. He'd been looking forward to at least sitting next to her, and now he couldn't even do that. Ah, well, he reflected as he dropped onto the sofa, he didn't want Emily for a quick affair. She was the one he wanted to spend the rest of his life with. And that being the case, he could afford to give her all the time she needed to reach the same conclusion.

"What's next on the agenda with that study?" he asked.

"This Saturday's the football game. We were going to try getting served in a restaurant without a reservation. We'll use the same format as before, with me starting out beautiful and uglying myself up later—although this time we're going to go back to my place to change. I refuse to go through another set of contortions in another public toilet stall."

Lucas chuckled. "I thought the results were kind of fetching."

Emily looked at him carefully. "You may be a variable we're going to have to do something about."

"But I'm not the least bit variable," he objected with a level look that gave her pause. She had the strangest feeling that they were talking about two entirely dif-

ferent things. She shook the impression off and continued, "If the maître d' sees you, he could react to you
instead of to my physical appearance."

"I'm not staying home," he said flatly.

"You don't have to. The restaurant's waiting area
should be jam-packed with people. You can stand off
to one side while I approach the reservations desk myself."

"That sounds—" He shot to his feet at the sound of
a muffled boom from the kitchen. "What the hell!" He
moved in that direction.

"Wait!" Emily grabbed his arm.

"For what? Are you expecting an encore?"

"You can't go out there. You don't know what caused
it. It could have been a gas explosion."

"Not likely. The building's totally electric. It has to
have been our pressure cooker."

"Yeah, but doing what?" Emily reluctantly trailed
along behind him.

"Take heart. There're a limited number of possibilities." He walked into the kitchen with Emily half a step
behind him.

"And none of them are good," she muttered.

"Where's our pot?" He looked over at the stove. It
was bare.

"I wish you wouldn't keep saying 'our.' That blasted
thing is all yours. You bought it and you—" She paused
as a small blob of a whitish substance landed on her
shoulder. She automatically looked up. The stew was
now plastered across the white ceiling. There was also
an indentation directly above the stove.

"Dammit!" Lucas jumped out of the way as a pulverized hunk of meat succumbed to the law of gravity.

"There goes your security deposit. You know, if you had been working over the stove, you could have been decapitated."

"At the very least," he said ruefully. "I wonder what I did wrong?"

"I'd say stopping at the garage sale probably heads the list. Ah-hah!" She caught sight of the handle of the lid half hidden behind the stove. She picked it up and dropped it into the trash, hastily moving out of the way as more vegetables began to fall.

"Don't throw that out," Lucas objected. "I want it."

"Sorry." She found the pot under the breakfast bar and tossed it after the lid. "My religion expressly forbids me to help anyone commit suicide, especially demented people."

"But—"

"Which is what you'd be if you were stupid enough to try that thing again."

Lucas sighed mournfully. "I guess you're right. And look at this mess we've got to clean up."

"We? This is your kitchen. Therefore, by transference, it's your mess."

"Emily McGregor! You wouldn't leave me alone with this, would you?"

Emily laughed at his horrified expression. "What's it worth to you?"

"My undying gratitude?" he asked hopefully.

"Try something more substantial."

"How about twenty quarts of freshly picked raspberries?" he offered craftily. "We could try making some jam to go with your applesauce."

Emily's covetous streak took over. She loved raspberries and they were very hard to find fresh. "Or we could freeze them. You really can get them?"

"Your suspicions wound me deeply." His melodramatic pose was ruined when he had to jump out of the way of more raining veggies. "One of my students operates a truck garden. He offered to sell them to me."

"It's a deal." Emily beamed happily at him.

9

LUCAS WHISTLED when Emily opened her apartment door in response to his ring. "Emily, you bring a whole new meaning to the word *beautiful*." *And whole new dimensions to frustration*, he thought, following her into the living room where he sank down onto the sofa in an attempt to hide his body's instinctive response to her feminine curves, which were barely covered by the sliver of scarlet silk she wore.

"I thought this outfit was rather effective, too," she said with satisfaction.

Fascinated, Lucas watched as she ran her fingers through her gleaming ebony curls and then leaned closer to the antique mirror above the breakfront to check the evenness of the brilliant red she'd applied to her lips.

Lips that he ached to feel against his again. His hands clenched into fists as he fought a silent battle with himself for control of his body. His overwhelming instinct was to fling her down on the sofa, dispose of that delectable bit of scarlet provocation and explore the body beneath it—to lose himself in her. Lucas swallowed dryly. If he didn't make love to her soon, he'd go stark raving mad.

He smiled inwardly at the image of himself running around the campus, babbling uncontrollably. Some of the students being as strange as they were, he doubted that he'd attract so much as a second glance.

But he was making progress with Emily, he consoled himself. She was totally at ease with him. She almost never tried to freeze him out the way she had in the beginning. And her reaction to their kisses . . . He shifted uncomfortably.

Emily glanced over her shoulder at him, frowning as she caught sight of his expression. He looked...pained, she finally decided. But why?

Maybe it was her dress? She studied the swell of her breasts above the low-cut neckline. A bit daring, but not overly so. Irritated, she decided to ask. "Why are you looking at me as if something were wrong?"

"Wrong?"

"If you were to tell me what's wrong, I'll try to fix it," she persisted. "The whole idea of this outfit is for me to attract attention."

"If you attract any more attention, they're liable to arrest you as an attractive nuisance," he said gruffly.

Emily blinked at the intensity of his tone. "Then why do you look so . . . ?" She waved her hand expressively.

"Because the sight of you brings all sorts of things to mind, none of them having anything to do with academic research."

"Oh," she murmured, having no trouble relating to what he was saying because the sight of him in his perfectly tailored gray suit was producing a similar reaction in her.

"You know, Lucas, this is all just window dressing." She gestured toward the dress. "It's not important. Not really."

"In one sense. But do you remember Christmastime when you were a kid?"

"Yes. Why?"

"How great the packages all looked wrapped up in shiny paper. The wrapping might not have changed what was inside the box, but it did add a certain allure and mystery to the whole thing. And a great deal of getting the present was the joy of unwrapping it." His voice dropped an octave. "And half the allure of that dress to a man is the fantasy of taking it off. Of discovering if your breasts are really as exquisitely shaped as they appear, if your hips are as smooth and rounded as they seem and if your legs really are that long and firm."

Emily felt her skin burn and a dull throbbing sensation began deep in her abdomen. Inundated by the desire flooding her, she closed her eyes in an attempt to think. What he was saying was all wrong. Deep in her heart, she knew it. Her body wasn't perfect. It was flawed. Fatally flawed. She couldn't let Lucas continue to think that she was perfect, she realized in panic. She had to tell him the truth before she got any more deeply involved with him. Or him with her.

She opened her mouth, but the damning words refused to come. Instead, an image of his face formed in her mind, its lean features hardened in rejection. She couldn't do it. She just couldn't say the words that would put that look on his face. And there was no need, she assured herself. While she didn't have the slightest doubt that Lucas was inexorably moving them both toward an affair, he had said absolutely nothing to make her believe that he had anything permanent in mind. And even if she'd completely miscalculated and he was thinking in terms of permanency, from what Marcy had said, it was highly unlikely that Lucas wanted children, or he would already have had them by now.

"I'm definitely going to have to work on it." Lucas's rueful voice interrupted her tortured thoughts.

"What?" Emily struggled to follow what he was saying.

"My technique. Telling you that I want to take off your clothes is not supposed to send you into a trance."

Emily grinned at him. "Where is it supposed to send me?"

He gave her a boyishly hopeful look that was totally at odds with the explosive glow of sexual desire she could see burning deep in his eyes.

"Into my arms?" he suggested.

Firmly, Emily beat down an impulse to do just that. To throw herself against his chest and kiss him until neither of them could think of anything but each other. But she couldn't do that. There wouldn't be another home game for another three weeks—too late for Marcy's preliminary study. And she owed Marcy, because if it hadn't been for Marcy and her study, she never would have met Lucas in the first place.

"Work first, play later," she finally said, picking up her red sequined evening purse.

"Is that a promise?" Lucas decided to gamble.

Emily studied his features, her gaze lingering on the sensual curve of his lips. And an appalling thought surfaced out of her subconscious: *I love him.* She had committed the ultimate folly. *No,* she instantly countered, falling in love with someone as lovable as Lucas

Sheridan was not folly; it was inevitable. And that being so, she might as well enjoy it while she could. She released the breath she'd unconsciously been holding and said, "A promise if you wish." Her heart jerked at the sudden flare of light in his eyes.

"Oh, I wish, my darling Emily. If I had three wishes, they'd all be for you."

Emily blinked, taken aback by the seriousness of his tone. For one brief second, doubt about the wisdom of allowing their relationship to deepen shook her, but she determinedly banished it. She refused to spoil what she did have by worrying about something that might never happen.

"Let's go strike a blow for academic research," she reminded in an attempt to defuse the sexually charged atmosphere. "Would you drive? These spike heels make it hard to work the car's pedals."

"I should think they'd play havoc with the tendons in your legs, too."

"I don't know about that, but I do know they aren't the least bit comfortable," Emily admitted. "But very high heels are supposed to be sexy."

"Says who?"

"Probably some man." She walked out the door he held open for her, pausing to make sure that the lock had caught behind them. "Men seem to make all the rules."

"Ha! Haven't you heard that the hand that rocks the cradle rules the world?"

Emily laughed. "As I recall, some man said that, too. Now, remember," she hurried on when he opened his mouth to argue, "when we get to the restaurant you aren't to let the maître d' catch sight of you."

"I'll try, but I still don't see how the restaurant can be all that busy."

"You will," Emily promised.

Emily was right. The reception area of the restaurant was packed with well-dressed, would-be diners. Most of whom were also sporting sunburned faces as souvenirs of the afternoon's football game.

Lucas used his body to shield her as they made their way through the crowded doorway. He looked around in astonishment. "I wouldn't have believed it, but you were correct. Where are all these people staying?"

"Try to get a motel room within a fifty-mile radius of the campus and you'll find out." She stood on tiptoe and peered over the heads of the milling people.

"I think I'll have a better view of the maître d' if I'm over there by the rest rooms," Lucas said. "Why don't you give me a couple of minutes to get into position."

"Good idea," Emily approved. "Once I've actually talked to him, we'll meet back in the parking lot, okay?"

Lucas gave her a thumbs-up sign and moved away. Emily waited a few moments and then began the slow process of working her way through the mass of bodies.

"Excuse me," she murmured as she inched around a very portly man.

"Would you mind—" He turned in annoyance, and Emily watched dispassionately as his eyes widened at the sight of her. "Of course, I'll excuse you, little lady," he revised expansively. "I'd forgive anyone as gorgeous as you are anything."

"Thank you," Emily answered dryly, more amused than irritated by the lust that sat so oddly on his pudgy face. Her amusement, however, quickly vanished when she felt his fingers pinch her thigh as she moved past him. Emily pressed her lips together angrily. Much as she wanted to jam her spike heel into his instep, the ensuing commotion would effectively ruin their research. So she contented herself with giving him a glare that promised retribution if she ever ran across him again.

By the time she'd reached the maître d' a few minutes later, she felt pummeled. She took a deep breath, checked to make sure that Lucas was in place, and tried to remember what Catherine had said about thinking yourself into a role.

You are Marilyn Monroe, Marilyn Monroe, Marilyn Monroe, she chanted to herself. Squaring her shoulders, she swayed toward the maître d', watching in satisfaction as a dark red flush surged up his thin neck.

"Good evening, sir." Emily gave him her best seductive smile.

The man gulped. "Yes? May I help you?"

"Oh, I do hope so." Her throaty whisper sent his Adam's apple bobbing. "I'm simply starved, and silly little me forgot to make reservations."

"Anyone as beautiful as you doesn't need to remember things," he replied. "How many are in your party?"

"Just me."

"Then you shall have the next table that is free, Miss—" He looked inquiringly at her.

"Handley, Marcy Handley. Thank you so much. I'll just go powder my nose while I'm waiting." Emily gave him another brilliant smile as a reward and, ignoring the disgruntled expressions of the people close enough to have overheard the exchange, made her escape.

"I don't think the poor devil knew what hit him," Lucas said as he caught up with her at the car. He unlocked the door, helped her in and then rounded the Porsche's gleaming hood.

"Actually," Emily pointed out, once Lucas had maneuvered the car out of the crowded parking lot, "I was afraid that I was going to be attacked by some of the waiting customers. Not that I'd have blamed them," she added judiciously. "It must be very frustrating to play by the rules and wait your turn and then get pushed out of the way by someone else who simply was born with a combination of features that your society happens to consider beautiful."

"A lot of effort went into the way you look tonight." Lucas deftly shifted gears as he passed a truck.

"True, but as Marcy pointed out when she roped me into this research, all the makeup in the world won't turn an attractive woman into a beautiful one." Emily sighed. "You know, Lucas, this whole study is kind of depressing."

"How so?" He flipped on his turn signal and pulled into the lane leading to her apartment.

"It just doesn't seem right that a random gift from a capricious fate should make such a difference."

"But it isn't just beauty that's random. Intelligence is also randomly distributed, and you must admit that clever people go much further than stupid ones. And charm, on occasion, can get you further than beauty and brains combined."

"True," Emily admitted. "Don't mind me. I guess I'm just feeling guilty."

Lucas reached over and squeezed her knee. "Don't. I've yet to meet anyone with less cause to feel guilty."

Emily ducked her head in shamed frustration. If only he knew how seriously she had lied by simply not telling him one very important thing about herself. She glanced furtively at him. He looked indulgent, but how would he look if he knew her secret?

There was no point in dwelling on something she couldn't change. But even if she couldn't change the fact of her sterility, she could at least try to tell him about it. But she just couldn't do it. There had been so much pain in her life these past few months, she just couldn't face the risk of adding still more.

The evening light was beginning to fade as Lucas parked his car next to hers. Emily eyed the brilliant red sky with appreciation. "I love the sunset."

Lucas shrugged. "All that color is caused by impurities in the atmosphere."

"I swear that more pleasure is spoiled by facts," she grumbled.

He gave her a mock leer as he opened the door to her apartment building. "On the contrary, facts can enhance one's pleasure considerably. For example, the sight of your body moving beneath that excuse for a dress brings to mind all kinds of facts."

Emily stopped fishing in her purse for her key and smiled at him. "The look in your eye brings to mind warnings, not facts." She turned her attention back to locating her key.

"Darling Emily." The gentle note in his voice made her look up. "I keep telling you that I'd never do anything to hurt you."

Emily stared into his eyes, distracted by the excitement she could see simmering just below their surface—an excitement that found an echoing cord in her.

Lucas reached out and gently tucked a stray curl behind her right ear. His touch sent her pulse racing.

"Emily, I—"

Emily watched in confusion as his features suddenly tightened as if he were in pain, and he jerked around.

"Be careful! You'll hurt him!" Mrs. Kitchener's elderly voice accused.

"Hurt him!" Lucas shook his leg, dislodging the snarling dog. "That vicious little brute just bit me!"

"It's not poor Everard's fault." Emily's neighbor scooped up her pet just as he was about to go on the attack again. "I got him from the pound," she confided.

"The pound?" Emily asked when Lucas simply stared at the old woman.

"Yes, indeed." Mrs. Kitchener nodded her white head. "He was abandoned, you know, and that undoubtedly caused irreparable harm to his emerging psyche."

"Is she acquainted with Marcy?" Lucas questioned Emily in an audible aside.

Emily shook her head, afraid that if she tried to say anything the laughter bubbling inside her would break out.

"Then I vote we introduce them," he said. "Marcy can practice on that hell-born beast."

"Everard is not a hell-born anything!" Mrs. Kitchener declared in outraged tones. "He was merely a tad too aggressive. He probably thought that you were attacking poor Emily. Didn't you, my precious baby?" Everard's mistress patted his woolly head. "You're such a clever boy." With a final smile for the wooden-faced Emily and the astounded Lucas, she continued on down the hall.

Emily hurriedly unlocked her door and pushed it open. She barely made it inside before she broke out laughing.

"What are you laughing about?" Lucas closed the door with a decided bang.

Emily stared into his outraged face and laughed all the harder. "If you could have just seen your expression when she said that poor Everard was a victim of his environment."

"You have a very macabre sense of humor." Lucas limped over to her sofa and plopped down.

"I'm sorry." She made a valiant, but not very effective, effort to be serious. "Let me see your wound."

"That isn't necessary," he said with an injured dignity that almost sent her into gales of laughter again.

"Are you going to sulk?" she teased.

"I never sulk!"

"You could have fooled me. Tell me, if you aren't sulking, why are you mad at me?"

"I'm not," he countered. "I'm mad at that monster masquerading as a dog, and I'm none too happy with his idiot keeper, either. But I can hardly say what I really think to an old lady."

"Probably not, although I'm beginning to feel that someone should." She walked over to her sideboard and poured a generous measure of whiskey into a cut-glass tumbler and handed it to him. "Here. Drown your pain in alcohol while I have a look at your wound."

"That's not necessary." He took a healthy swallow of the whiskey. "You need to change so we can get back to the restaurant before the crowd thins out."

"It'll be packed until after ten. I called earlier to check, and they're booked solid until closing."

Emily squatted on the floor in front of him. She took his shoe off, lifted his foot onto the coffee table and, pushing up his pant leg, gently pulled down his charcoal-gray sock.

Her fingers brushed against the dark hair on his leg, making it hard for her to concentrate on what she was supposed to be doing. All she could think about was what she wanted to do, and that was to touch him—to explore the texture of his skin and the feel of the muscles beneath it. Determinedly, she blanked out her own reactions and finished pulling his sock off.

She winced when she saw his ankle.

"Well? Will I live?"

"Not if you don't stay away from surly-tempered little beasts. His teeth broke the skin in four places. It didn't bleed much, but you're going to have some nasty bruising there."

"Maybe if we accused him of having rabies, the Humane Society would impound him for a couple of weeks while they wait to see if he comes down with it," Lucas suggested hopefully.

Emily rocked back on her heels and considered his idea. "I could be wrong, but I don't think they wait for the animal to develop signs of the disease. I think they examine its brain tissue."

Lucas frowned. "But to do that, they'd have to—"

"Quite true. But it's all irrelevant, anyway. The monster's up-to-date on his immunizations."

"How do you know that?"

"Because you aren't his only victim. He got me a couple of months ago and, when I complained, Mrs. Kitchener told me that there was nothing to worry about because he'd had all his shots. That's what that little red heart dangling from his collar signifies."

"I didn't suppose it stood for love!"

"But you really should have a tetanus shot," Emily continued. "Puncture wounds can cause some nasty infections, and heaven only knows what he's had his teeth in lately."

"You mean *who* he's had his teeth into. Don't worry. I had a tetanus shot in the spring. They're good for years."

"Then I guess that all that's left to do is to kiss it and make it better." Emily leaned over and placed a featherlight kiss on one of the bluish marks. Enchanted by the feel of his skin, she placed another kiss beside the first and then began to string kisses around his ankle like beads on a necklace.

Lucas jerked as if he'd been struck.

"Emily, what are you doing?"

She gave him a sultry smile. "You must not have been listening. I told you, I'm kissing it better. Although, I suppose we really ought to put some ice on it to cut down on the swelling."

"I think a certain amount of swelling is inevitable when you're around," he muttered with a wry glance down at his lap.

Emily's eyes automatically followed his to the sight of his manhood straining against the material of his pants. A surge of awareness of herself as a desirable and desired woman shortened her breathing.

"I'll go get the ice." She got to her feet and escaped into the kitchen. Once there, she took a deep, steadying breath and then opened the small freezer compartment above her refrigerator. She frowned when she saw all the raspberries, only then remembering that she'd taken the ice trays out so as to have more room for the fruit.

She swung the freezer drawer closed and glanced around the kitchen as if seeking inspiration. "Of course," she said, seeing the kitchen sink.

Hurrying back into the living room, she announced, "I haven't got any ice, but I have another idea. We'll soak your ankle in cold water."

"I have an even better idea," he countered. "Let's let it swell and pretend we don't notice."

"Nonsense. All that's needed is a little determination. Come into the bathroom, and I'll run the water in the tub for you."

With a resigned grimace, Lucas got to his feet and limped after her. "I have the distinct feeling that this is going to be one of those cures that's worse than the disease," he grumbled, but Emily ignored him. If he didn't have the sense to take care of his body, she did. She had plans for it. Oh, did she have plans for it! A smile of anticipation curved her lips.

When they reached the bathroom, she turned to find Lucas a bare inch from her. The soft, clingy silk of her dress swirled against the gray material of his suit pants, seeming to draw him even closer.

"Umm." Emily cleared her throat and inched backward. "You pull your pant leg up, and I'll run the water." She flipped on the faucet, trying to concentrate on what she was doing. It was impossible. She was much more interested in what she was feeling. Giving up, she decided to opt for simply getting the job done as quickly as possible. She took a thick towel down from the rack, folded it and set it on the edge of the tub.

"Sit on the towel while you soak." She turned off the tap.

Lucas eyed the water consideringly for a long moment and then shook his head. "Not a good idea. What if the water splashes and I get my pants wet? Then we'll have to go to my place so I can change, and we'll never get back to the restaurant in time."

"You're right. You'd better take them off first."

"Now, that's an idea." Lucas gave her a slow, sensual smile that left her in no doubt as to what she was inviting, but she didn't care. She wanted him. Wanted him with a need that had long since passed rational thought.

Mesmerized, she watched as his long fingers quickly unbuckled his belt and thrust his zipper down with an impatient jerk. He hastily stepped out of his trousers, and Emily found her attention riveted to the bulge of his masculinity against his shorts. With a monumental effort to appear a whole lot more sophisticated than she felt, Emily reached for the pants he handed her and turned to hang them on the hook on the back of the bathroom door.

Emily stared at the white painted wood, trying to regain her sense of equilibrium while she listened to the sound of Lucas stepping into the water.

"Tell me, do you also have a handy home remedy for hypothermia?" he complained.

Emily turned and covered the scant yard that separated them. "It can't be that cold," she remarked, trying to remain impersonal.

"It's worse. This is definitely not one of your more inspired ideas."

Oh, I don't know about that, Emily thought as her eyes strayed to the skin of his tanned thighs. Against the whiteness of his shirttails, it seemed infinitely touchable.

"Feel it," he insisted.

With her eyes focused on what she really wanted to feel, Emily absently stuck a hand into the water, gasping when the icy liquid jarred her out of her sensual preoccupation. He was right. It really was cold, and making him sick was not her intention.

"Maybe we should just soak a towel in the water and wrap the towel around your ankle?" she finally suggested.

"Maybe we should just forget the whole thing." Lucas stepped out of the tub, and Emily suddenly felt dwarfed. "I have another idea to take my mind off my battle wound."

"Yes?" She couldn't drag her eyes away from the long expanse of his bare legs.

"Yes, what?" he asked softly. "Yes, you feel the same way I do? Yes, you feel as if you might shatter into a million tiny pieces if I don't touch you?" His fingers traced over her left collarbone before coming to rest at the base of her throat where a wild pulse beat. "Yes, you find me just as fascinating as I find you?" His hand suddenly slipped into the plunging neckline of her dress to find and cup her small breast. "Yes, you—"

Emily gasped, twisting beneath his caressing fingers. "Yes, you talk too much," she murmured, pulling his head down to hers.

Lucas reacted with flattering swiftness to her invitation. His mouth captured hers; his breath mixed with hers. This time his kiss wasn't tentative; it was hard and hungry, as if he were starved for the taste of her. His tongue surged inside, deepening the intimacy.

Emily shuddered. She felt as if she had finally discovered exactly what she'd been created for.

Lucas pulled her closer with one hand while the other found the zipper at the back of her dress. Her breathing became shallower as anticipation spiraled through her.

"You smell so good, my darling Emily. Like a garden after a summer rain." He nuzzled the base of her neck, allowing his teeth to lightly graze her sensitive skin.

Emily felt dizzy, suffocated by the need flooding her mind. She moaned as his tongue flicked out to stroke where his teeth had been.

Lucas pulled down her dress, exposing her flesh to his devouring gaze.

"My God, Emily, you're so exquisitely formed." The tremor in his voice was reflected in the unsteadiness of his fingers as he reached out to reverently touch the tip of a breast, as if unable to deny himself any longer. He swung her up into his arms and carried her through to her bedroom where he gently placed her on the bed.

Emily waited in an agony of longing as he lowered his head. She was intoxicated by the look in his eyes as he stared at her breasts with a look of awe, desire and raw hunger, curiously mixed with reverence. It sent desire flowing through her veins. The thud of her rapid heartbeat filled her ears, deafening her to everything but her own needs. Finally, when she was light-headed with longing, he swooped lower, capturing the tip of her breast in his mouth.

Emily's whole body clenched and she grasped his head, her fingers clutching convulsively at his soft hair.

Lucas gently suckled on her breast, and Emily groaned as a liquid fire began to loosen the taut muscles of her abdomen.

"Lucas, please, I can't . . . I want . . ."

"The exact same thing I want." He suddenly stood.

Emily watched with half-closed eyes as he unbuttoned his shirt. A wild sense of exultation filled her as she took in his nervous, uncoordinated movements. Lucas was every bit as affected by her as she was by him. Her gaze narrowed as he pulled his shirt off and dropped it to the floor. He had a wide, heavily muscled chest, thickly covered by a dark cloud of hair that arrowed down to disappear into his shorts—shorts he quickly removed.

Her heart almost stopped, then lurched into an erratic rhythm at the sight of him standing naked in front of her. He looked like some primitive being, elemental and untamed.

Emily tensed as Lucas lifted her and with one deft movement pulled her dress down over her hips. Carelessly, he tossed it behind him. Her half-slip quickly followed. As if fascinated by the sight of her creamy skin, he ran his finger above the waistband of her panty hose.

Emily's skin seemed to flutter beneath the friction of his hand, which dipped lower to stroke over her stomach, then came to rest on the sensitive area between her legs. She could feel the heat pooling in her abdomen and she wiggled restively, trying to slow the feeling down. She wanted to savor it, to relish each exquisite sensation.

Lucas slipped his hands beneath the elastic waistband and slowly began to peel her panty hose downward. His mouth followed their slow descent as he rained kisses over her quivering flesh. He paused a moment when his wandering mouth reached the tops of her legs, and he gently bit on the skin of her inner thigh.

Emily could feel herself softening and opening to him. She couldn't stand much more of this. She wanted to feel him inside her.

"Lucas, please... You're driving me crazy. I want you now." She tossed her head restlessly and her black curls tumbled across the white pillowcase, reflecting the wild, uncontrolled desire that engulfed her. She held out her arms to him in a welcome as old as time itself.

"Emily, if I do that, I won't be able to control—"

"Good," she replied, pulling him down to her and wantonly arching her body against his. "That way, neither of us will be in control."

"My darling, darling Emily." His gaze held hers as his hand slipped between them and his finger probed her soft dampness. His eyes warmed with satisfaction as he realized just how ready for him she was.

He braced himself above her as he carefully positioned his body.

"Lucas!" Emily cried as an overwhelming sense of urgency filled her. She grasped his shoulders and tried to pull him forward. Finally, with a powerful surge, he filled her and Emily gasped, transfixed by his possession. For a brief second her body struggled to accept his maleness, loosening and stretching around his burning hardness. Then her muscles seemed to contract about him, and she was the one holding him captive to her femininity.

"Ah, Emily," he groaned, and Emily stared up into his face. His eyes were curiously blank as if his mind were focused on some inner vision only he could see.

Emily tugged demandingly on his shoulders until he refocused on her, his lips lifting in a smile of such promise that she felt cherished.

"My Emily." He slowly lowered himself until she could feel the heavy weight of him in every cell of her body. Lucas slowly rubbed his hair-covered chest over the tips of her breasts, and she trembled at the sensation.

"Lucas!" she panted.

"Emily," he responded in a voice that shook. He raised his body far enough for him to capture her distended nipple in his mouth.

She grasped his shoulders and wrapped her slim legs around his waist, forcing him deeper. Her skin was burning and she felt frantic with need.

In answer to her unspoken plea, he began to move— slowly at first and then with increasing speed. The hot rhythm quickly sent her over the edge into a spasm of ecstasy so intense that she barely noticed when Lucas followed her. Her body felt boneless and she closed her eyes, the better to savor the sensations and the joy of being one with the man she loved.

10

EMILY SQUEEZED PAST the people trying to enter the restaurant and emerged into the soft, September night air. She walked slowly toward their parked car as she waited for Lucas to follow her out.

Her heartbeat quickened as he appeared in the brightly lit doorway. The outside spotlight fell on him, adding a reddish gleam to his dark hair. Emily's fingertips tingled as she remembered its texture as she'd held his head against her breast. She could recall the exact feel of the weight of him as he'd covered her trembling body with his. Then she frowned as Lucas was accosted by the Goodmans, who had exited the restaurant immediately behind him. All she wanted to do was to spend what remained of the weekend making love with Lucas—to express what she felt physically, since she couldn't express it verbally. But what did Lucas feel?

As if searching for an answer, she studied him with painful intensity. His head was tilted slightly to one side as he listened politely to Mrs. Goodman.

Lucas had exquisite manners, she acknowledged, but she'd long since realized that they were only a veneer for the real personality beneath; a veneer she was certain he'd acquired as a prerequisite for a successful career in business. Underneath all that surface politeness lay a streak of determination and ruthlessness the depth of which she could only begin to guess at.

She also knew for certain that Lucas was no immature man needing to prove his masculinity by bedding every attractive woman he met. Lucas might not love her as she loved him, but he cared about her. He liked her as a person, respected her as a teacher and desired her as a woman. A shiver of excitement ran through her at the memory of how he'd expressed his desire for her. He hadn't made love to her with the practiced technique of a man who'd had a great deal of experience. In fact—a tender smile curved her lips at the thought— he hadn't shown much technique at all. Just a vast, burning need for her.

"At last." The sound of Lucas's voice made her jump and she turned to him, grateful to shelve all the problems for which she had no answer.

"Mrs. Goodman is a dear old thing, but once she gets talking, it's almost impossible to shut her up without giving offense."

"I know," Emily sympathized. "I've had that problem a few times myself."

"And I could hardly tell her that you were lurking out here in the shrubbery or she might have decided to include you in the conversation. And I could just see us trying to explain why you look like a bag lady on her night out." He grinned at her. "At least I didn't have to worry about some man making off with you while you're dressed like that."

"Men don't make off with me, no matter how I'm dressed," she retorted. "I have a mind of my own."

"It's not the mind that causes the problems." He took her arm and started toward the car. "You know, Emily, having met you, I'm beginning to have a great deal of sympathy for Arab countries, which make a woman wear a veil when she goes outside."

"This getup is much more effective than a veil," Emily pointed out. "It virtually renders me invisible."

"You still walk with the same lithe grace," he said reflectively. "My blood pressure shoots up fifty points just watching you move across the room."

Emily stole a quick glance at him as he opened the car door for her. His face was set in thoughtful lines. He didn't appear to be teasing her; in fact he looked dead serious. She bit her lip in sudden uncertainty. Maybe she should make a greater effort to tell him about her sterility? But how could she do that now? After they'd made love? It would seem as if she were fishing for some kind of long-term commitment from him. As if she were trying to use the fact that they'd made love to pressure him into something that he hadn't suggested himself. And she couldn't bear for him to think that she was the type of woman who bartered her favors for gain.

Sheridan, you're a heavy-handed fool. He berated himself as he saw Emily's face cloud over. Things had been going so well and then he had to go and upset her with his talk of hiding her away from the world. Slamming her car door shut in self-disgust, he clenched his car keys in his fist as he headed toward the driver's side. He welcomed the bite of the keys in his hand to break him out of the sensual haze in which Emily seemed to unconsciously ensnare him. And it was unconscious, he recognized. From the very beginning, she'd been more interested in keeping him at arm's length than in attracting him; but even so he'd managed to slip through her formidable reserve and reach the vibrant woman behind it. His body hardened as he remembered just how far behind her reserve he'd gotten. Tonight had been the most fantastic experience of his life. He had heard the expression "losing oneself in another person," but until Emily, he'd never experienced it. And having experienced it, he wanted nothing more than to rush her home and repeat the experience—all night long. But he was afraid to.

He shoved his key into the ignition and twisted it, deriving some small satisfaction when the powerful engine roared to life. He knew he didn't dare rush her. He needed to give her time to become accustomed to their being lovers. Then he'd gradually introduce the idea of marriage, and before you knew it, they'd be living in the suburbs with a couple of kids and a dog. He chuckled. Just so long as the animal bore no resemblance to that monster of Mrs. Kitchener's.

"What's so funny?" she asked.

"Do you like dogs?"

"Dogs?" Emily blinked uncertainly at his question.

"Yes. Dogs. Do you like them?"

"I always did until I met Everard. Why?"

"Just curious." He checked the traffic and pulled into the busy street. "We did this backward."

Emily frowned, not understanding. "How so?"

"Since we were reasonably certain that you wouldn't get a seat in your unattractive mode . . ."

"And we were right." She shivered expressively. "That maître d' took one look at me and couldn't get rid of me fast enough."

"Yes, but in your attractive mode he fell over himself to fit you in. So what we should have done was to have tried out the disguise first and the normal look second. Then we could have taken the table he would have found and right now we'd be eating."

"Yeah." Emily grimaced. "I'm starved, too."

"Let's stop on the way home and get something. Every place can't still be packed. It's after nine-thirty. I'd even settle for a pizza."

"You're on. Swing by my apartment and I'll change."

"Why waste the time? Unless that bodysuit is uncomfortable?"

"It's not uncomfortable, but I look awful."

"Does it matter what anyone else thinks?" he asked.

"Not to me," she admitted, "although I would prefer not to have to make any long-winded explanations if we run into someone I know."

"Explanations can be tedious," he agreed. "Tell you what, why don't we go through the drive-in window of that Mexican restaurant over by the mall. There's a menu in the glove compartment."

Emily opened the glove compartment and began to rummage through it, looking for the menu. Near the bottom she found a thick book. Curious, she pulled it out and read the title, *Alcoholism and Its Effect on the Family.*

"I saw that in the bookstore the other day, and I thought I'd take a look at it," he said defensively.

"Ahh, there's the menu." Emily deliberately changed the subject. Lucas didn't want to talk about the book and there was no reason he should. Her goal had been to get him to look at his father's role in his family objectively, and reading that book should be a great first step. Hopefully, Lucas's innate curiosity and sense of fair play would do the rest.

"JUST A MINUTE and I'll—" Marcy looked up, amazed by the sight of Emily standing in her office doorway.

"Good Lord, Emily! That getup is fantastic! You look positively disgusting. I love it!"

Emily laughed. "Have you got a minute? I need a cold drink and a kind word before I feel up to facing the world again."

"Sure. Come in and rest your feet. Is a soda okay?"

"Sounds like manna from heaven." Emily sighed as she slipped off her beat-up oxfords and wiggled her feet in their thick cotton tights on the cool linoleum floor. "It's so hot out there. I swear it feels more like July than late September."

Marcy handed her a chilled can and studied Emily's face as she took a long, thirsty swallow.

"Where'd you get that appalling makeup?" she demanded.

"From a friend over in the theater department. She also suggested that I wear this shade of grayish-beige because it drains all the color out of my skin."

"It certainly does. You look like you died three days ago. Where were you today?"

Emily grimaced. "Riding the bus. Yesterday I went as myself and today I went like this."

"And what did you find out?"

Emily frowned. "Not what I'd expected. It would seem that no one is willing to give up his seat on a bus."

Marcy echoed Emily's frown. "No one? Not even as your normal self?"

"Nope. Men looked at my body, but they were very careful to avoid eye contact."

"Probably to avoid recognizing you as a human being with needs that might run counter to their own comfort," Marcy suggested.

"Lucas made an interesting observation. He pointed out that in the first two experiments we did—trying to return something and trying to get a seat in a restaurant—the people agreeing to those things weren't actually giving me anything of their own. But in the bus, they would have had to give up their seat."

Marcy paused reflectively. "He could be on to something, there. It's certainly a factor worth exploring in the actual study." She shot Emily a calculating glance. "Lucas seems to be a very perceptive man."

"Uh-huh."

Emily's voice had softened, and Marcy felt a flare of triumph. She'd been right: Lucas was exactly what Emily had needed to shake her out of the depression her operation had plunged her into.

"I take it he was with you on the bus today?" Marcy asked, trying for more information. "You should have brought him along."

"He had a class to teach. He takes his teaching very seriously."

"Give him time. He'll mellow out."

Emily frowned. "I don't think so. He's a very intense kind of person. What he does, he does in meticulous detail and with total concentration."

Marcy chortled. "Now that sounds like a man with possibilities."

To her dismay, Emily felt a flush warm her cheeks. Praying that her stage makeup was heavy enough to hide the fact, she changed the subject. Marcy was much too astute. She didn't want her probing into her relationship with Lucas. It was still too new and precious to share with anyone.

"Marcy, I want your professional opinion on something."

"Sure, shoot." Marcy leaned back in her swivel chair and propped her disreputable sneakers on a pile of papers on her desk.

"If someone is fascinated with various methods of pain and torture—"

"Not Lucas!" Marcy shot up in her seat, scattering papers in all directions. "What did he do to you?"

"Lucas?" Emily blinked in surprise. "What does Lucas have to do with it? He's in the School of Business, not the history department."

Marcy leaned over and started gathering up the scattered papers. She flung them carelessly back on her desk and then studied Emily's perplexed features.

"Emily," Marcy said slowly, "you'd tell me if something were wrong, wouldn't you?"

"It all depends, but in this case you seem to have gotten hold of the wrong end of the stick. Believe me, there's nothing the least bit kinky about Lucas. My problem is with a graduate student. I mentioned him once before. He—"

Emily reached into her briefcase and extracted a blue folder with the university's emblem emblazoned on it in silver. She handed it to Marcy and said, "Read a page or so of this and tell me what you think."

Marcy read, her eyes widening with disbelief as she progressed down the page. "My God—" she breathed the words like a prayer "—did the Indians really do things like that to the settlers?"

"Yes, and the settlers reciprocated," Emily informed her. "The eighteenth century was a violent time. So violent, in fact, that I don't think my stomach is going to last the distance. This guy's preoccupation with various forms of torture seems almost . . ." Emily gestured impotently.

"Sick? Scary?" Marcy filled in. "I certainly wouldn't go down any dark alleys with him. Neither would I give him any small animals for pets."

"You think he's dangerous?"

"I doubt it. There's no real proof that reading or writing about something antisocial makes you more likely to do it yourself." Marcy shrugged. "If it did, Agatha Christie would have been a mass murderess. I mean, consider it. That woman killed off more Englishmen than World War I."

"I suppose. It's just that his paper gives me the creeps."

"I know what you mean. He seems to be wallowing in it. I get no sense of professional detachment."

"That's it!" Emily nodded decisively. "That's what's been bothering me. I just couldn't put my finger on it."

"What are you going to do about it?" Marcy handed the folder back.

"I'm not sure. Probably just get nightmares. The student is male and the other faculty members on the committee are also male. If I object, chances are good they'll band together and have a hearty laugh about the squeamish little woman in their midst." Emily paused as she suddenly remembered some of Lucas's reactions to the things she said and did. They didn't come any more masculine than Lucas Sheridan, and yet he almost never responded in a chauvinistic manner.

"What's the matter?" Marcy asked.

"I was just thinking. You know, Marcy, I'm beginning to fear that all the put-downs I've had to endure from some of the men in this university have made me just as bigoted as they are."

Marcy snorted. "That'll be the day!"

"No, I'm serious. I hadn't realized it before I met Lucas, but I've developed the habit of transferring the prejudices of a few men to all men. What I just said about that committee is a perfect example. I may have good reason to suspect that that's what they'll do, but I won't really know until I put it to the test." Emily stuffed the folder back into her briefcase. "At the next committee meeting, I'm going to be honest about how I feel about this proposal and see what happens."

"Lots of luck, but I'd be very leery of judging all men by Lucas. In my opinion, he's unique. What's the next thing you two have scheduled for my study? I've only got another couple of weeks before I need to get started analyzing your data."

Emily got to her feet. "I'm going to fill in for the receptionist at the plastics factory on Thursday and then we're going to try the bar on Friday night. I should have the first half of our report written up for you by tomorrow and the rest of it by the middle of next week."

"Good." Marcy walked her to the door. "I can hardly wait to read it. Be sure to let me know if there's anything I can do to help."

DESPITE EMILY'S good intentions, it was actually two days later before she finished keying their conclusions from the first half of the study into her computer. She pressed the Print key and began to gather up the papers she'd been grading. She'd drop the report off at Marcy's office on her way to the departmental staff meeting. Then Marcy could begin to analyze the data before she and Lucas started the second part of the study tomorrow.

Anticipation sparked in Emily at the promise of a whole day spent with Lucas. Or, at least, working near Lucas. And then...she intended to lure him back to her apartment under the pretext of giving him a cooking lesson.

And then... A slow flush heated her skin and her stomach twisted in an agony of longing. Then she was going to seduce him. Not that it would take much effort. She grinned idiotically at her closed office door. Lucas reacted to her slightest encouragement like a starving man being flung a crust of bread. Never in her life had she felt so needed, so essential to someone's happiness. It was a heady experience.

For a brief moment, uncertainty flitted through her mind. Perhaps she was reading into his reactions the motivation she wanted. But she quickly banished the thought, refusing to go looking for trouble. She knew it was out there and in the end it would undoubtedly find her. In the meantime, she intended to relish what she could have.

The printer finished, and Emily was gathering up Marcy's report when the phone rang. She glanced at her watch. She had at most two minutes before she absolutely had to leave if she wasn't going to be late for the staff meeting. Hastily, she picked up the phone with one hand while she stuffed the report into her briefcase with the other.

"Dr. McGregor speaking."

"This is Dr. Warren's secretary," a crisp voice announced. "This afternoon's staff meeting has been canceled."

"Canceled?" Emily stopped stuffing and paid attention. "Why?"

"Dr. Warren was suddenly taken ill with the flu and had to go home."

"Thank you for letting me know." Emily absently hung up the phone while she contemplated her unexpectedly free afternoon. Her gaze dropped to the report and a hot flood of excitement poured through her. She'd use it as an excuse to see Lucas. She could tell him that she wanted to go over what she'd written before she gave it to Marcy. She reached for her phone to see if he was in his office.

To her delight, the secretary he shared with several of the other professors told her that Lucas had left for home directly after his nine o'clock class. Emily grabbed her briefcase and left. With the thought of Lucas drawing her like a magnet, she reached his apartment in record time.

"I thought you said you had a departmental meeting this afternoon?" He gestured her into the apartment.

"Dr. Warren's down with the flu that seems to be making the rounds on campus. Since I unexpectedly found myself free, I thought we could go over the report I just finished for Marcy." She looked eagerly at his lean features, then focused on the white smudge on his left cheek. *Flour,* she realized, as the heavenly aroma of baking bread finally penetrated her absorption with him. "Are you practicing your cooking?"

"Oh, a little," he said dismissively. "Why don't we sit down in the living room and go over the report. I'll—" He broke off as a timer sounded in the kitchen.

Emily eyed him curiously. "Whatever's in your oven is done," she finally said when he didn't move.

"Yes, why don't you have a seat and—"

"I'd rather see the results of your cooking." Emily walked past him into the kitchen. With reluctance visible in every line of his body, Lucas followed her.

"If you don't take whatever it is out, it's going to burn," she suggested when he simply stood there. "I promise not to make any snide cracks."

Lucas sighed and, opening the oven door, extracted a pan of large yeast rolls. Emily watched as he inverted the pan onto a plate and a thick, brown caramel sauce slowly trickled down over the sides of the oversize rolls. She frowned in confusion. She wasn't sure that she herself could produce such perfect-looking rolls. So how could Lucas—who exploded grapes and burned butter?

She looked up into his wary face and suddenly knew that she'd been had.

"You could cook all the time!" She gestured furiously toward the rolls. "Not only that, but from the look of it, you can cook better than I can." Anger burned in her chest in a hard, painful knot. "What was it?" she spat out. "Some kind of perverted joke?"

"No. Desperation," he said seriously. "I took one look at that picture of you that Marcy showed me and was inundated in hormones." He grimaced in self-disgust. "I felt like an adolescent who'd just discovered the centerfold in a men's magazine. I couldn't wait to get to know you so that I could find out if you were as fascinating inside as you were outside. And then I met you and it was immediately obvious that getting to know you was not going to be an easy matter. Every time I tried to set up a meeting, you stalled. You seemed—" he paused "—evasive."

Emily winced at the accuracy of his description.

When she made no comment, he continued, "So I thought that if I could relate to you in a role that you felt comfortable in, it would help. Since you were a teacher, teaching me something seemed the answer."

Emily felt the knot of anger begin to unravel at his obvious sincerity. She hadn't been the butt of a joke, after all.

"Let me get this straight. This whole cooking thing was simply a ploy to get to know me better?"

"Yes."

Emily glanced down at the steaming yeast rolls and her mouth watered hungrily. "And you can already cook?"

"Yes, I have a Cordon-Bleu certificate," he admitted, and then seemed to brace himself for her reaction.

"You what!" Her eyes widened in shock. "And you almost killed us with that pressure cooker?"

"We weren't even in the room," he argued. "And, besides, that accident wasn't staged. I'd never used one before, and I did follow the woman's directions exactly.

"Emily." Lucas reached out and cupped her chin. She could smell the faint aroma of yeast that still clung to his fingers.

"Emily, I never meant to hurt you. I swear. I—" He stopped before he blurted out that he loved her—that all he wanted was to marry her and spend the rest of his life with her. He knew it was too soon to be talking in terms of permanency. Not only was it too soon, but she was off balance because of his deception. He'd wait until they'd finished the research for Marcy, and then he'd discuss the future with her. In the meantime he'd work on consolidating his position in her life and her emotions.

"Please don't be mad," he cajoled.

"I'm not mad. In fact," she said slowly, "I think I'm flattered."

"You are?" he asked hopefully.

"But I'm not sure." Her frown was belied by the fugitive twinkle in her sapphire eyes.

"You definitely should be," he told her in all seriousness. "I've never in my life gone to such lengths to get

to know a woman, but you still deserve an apology."
He reached out and slowly undid the top button of her
blouse.

Emily swallowed at the kick of nervous excitement
that spiraled through her.

"What are you doing?" she asked, immediately
wincing at the inanity of the question.

"Apologizing." Three more buttons were pulled free.
"And you know what they say about actions speaking
louder than words."

"Umm." Emily was having trouble making sense of
any words as he pulled her blouse off and dropped it
onto the chair. He reached around her, deftly unfas-
tened her sheer beige bra and tossed it after the blouse.

Lucas leaned back and drew an unsteady breath at
the sight of her small, bare breasts. "You're so beautiful, Emily—" his voice was hushed "—like a Michelan-
gelo statue suddenly imbued with life."

His deeply tanned fingers hovered over her pale skin
and Emily shivered, finding the contrast deeply erotic.
She closed her eyes as he cupped one of her breasts and
rubbed the pad of his thumb over her nipple, convuls-
ing it into a hard bead of desire. He grasped it between
his fingertips and gently tugged. Bending his head, he
captured the other in his mouth. His tongue curled
around her throbbing flesh and Emily swayed forward, seeking more. She wanted to feel him, to taste
him, to experience his possession with a hunger that
obliterated everything else. Her hands went to his shirt,
and she tugged it free of his pants.

"Oh, yes," he whispered and yanked it over his head,
carelessly dropping it onto the kitchen floor. She placed

the palms of her hands on his waist and slowly pushed them upward, but the heat radiating from his body seemed to glue their flesh together. She flexed her fingers experimentally, smiling at the responding shudder that coursed through him. She found his violent reaction to her slightest touch a powerful stimulus to her own desire.

Lucas unzipped her skirt and pushed it and her silk slip to the floor, leaving her wearing only a pair of white bikini panties.

"You're magnificent." Lucas touched her abdomen with a finger that shook slightly and Emily gasped. She felt as if she'd just made contact with a live wire. She watched in an agony of longing as he roughly unzipped his pants and kicked them aside.

Scooping her up in his arms, he headed toward the bedroom.

Hungrily, Emily buried her face in his neck and flicked her tongue lightly over his skin. Its salty taste flooded her mouth. She breathed deeply, relishing the clean, faintly astringent aroma of his soap. When she gently bit his firm skin, his arms suddenly tightened around her. Emily smiled in satisfaction at the evidence of just how tenuous was Lucas's hold on his self-control.

His bedroom was nothing more than a blur to Emily as he carried her inside and dropped her onto the king-size bed. He followed her immediately. With a rough eagerness that she found intoxicating, he bent his head and licked the tip of her breast.

"Lucas!" she gasped. She thrust her fingers through his short hair and pulled him closer. His hot mouth closed over her breast and he suckled urgently.

When Emily moaned and arched into him, Lucas reacted instantly to her unspoken invitation, parting her legs with his knee and slipping between them. He captured her mouth and pressed, forcing her lips apart. His tongue and his manhood invaded her at the same time.

Emily's entire body clenched in a dizzying spasm of need. Frantically she pressed closer to him, as if trying to absorb him into the very essence of her being.

Slowly—much too slowly for her tortured senses—Lucas pushed forward and then retreated, creating a pleasure so intense it was almost a physical pain. Her body was one throbbing ache.

"Please, Lucas, I can't stand any more!"

"Yes," he murmured, increasing the momentum of his thrusts, quickly driving them both into a mindless shattering of the tension.

Slowly, ever so slowly, Emily's mind drifted down from where ecstasy had sent it. She wiggled slightly, glorying in the weight of his body, which was sprawled across hers. Lovingly she ran her fingers over his sweat-slicked skin and placed tiny kisses along his collarbone.

"I'm much too heavy for you," he gasped, rolling onto his side. Almost before she had time to mourn the loss of their intimacy, he pulled her back into his arms in a grip so tight she could feel his ribs pushing into her side.

"Every time I touch you I promise myself that I'm going to take hours and hours and make slow, languorous love to you, but then I touch you and all my good intentions shatter."

"I know." She laughed weakly. "I don't think there's anything even vaguely slow and languorous about the way we make each other feel."

"I have a plan," he told her, and his breath tickled her ear.

Emily tilted her head back, batted her eyelashes at him in a parody of Mae West and said, "Do tell. I'm all ears."

His devouring glance slid down her body. "Not by a long shot, you aren't. But you're distracting me. My plan is that now that the edge is off our need for each other, we should try again. This time, maybe we'll have better luck."

"Any better luck and I'll be dead," Emily whispered against his lips. It was her last rational thought for hours.

11

EMILY GLANCED AROUND the meticulously manicured landscaping in front of the factory's offices. The business looked a lot more prosperous than she'd anticipated.

"You're sure your friend doesn't mind us using his office for our research?" she asked dubiously.

Lucas reached around her and opened the smoked-glass doors. "No. George loves a good joke."

"Joke!" Emily raised her eyebrows in only partly assumed outrage. "I'll thank you to remember that this is serious scientific research. It's also turning out to be rather intriguing. I'm very curious as to what Marcy's completed study will show."

"I am, too," Lucas admitted. "Any successful businessman knows how important it is to project the right image, but I'd never really considered how it worked in everyday life before."

"Lucas! You old son of a gun!" A middle-aged man hurried toward them from across the reception area. Emily winced at the vigorous handshake the two men exchanged.

"So this is the little lady who's going to be my receptionist today?" He turned to Emily, his eyes widening as his gaze moved from her carefully tumbled mass of ebony curls down over her perfect features, past her severely cut black silk suit, over the sheer silk stockings that encased her slender legs, to her Italian leather shoes.

"Wow!" He whistled weakly. "You did her an injustice, Lucas. Beautiful doesn't begin to describe her."

"I can talk, too," Emily announced tartly.

"Sorry." George grinned sheepishly. "This is where you'll be working." He gestured around the room and Emily's glance followed. A thick beige carpet covered the floor, and comfortably upholstered chairs were arranged here and there to give the feeling of an elegant living room. In the center stood a large mahogany desk with a high-backed brown leather chair behind it for the receptionist.

"Very nice, George," Lucas approved. "You've certainly come up in the world since the first time we did business."

George sighed. "That was a lot of years ago. Margot and I had just founded the company, and she was trying to run the office and take care of our son while I was out on the road trying to get orders. And now our son's in college and Margot's been dead almost sixteen months."

Lucas squeezed his shoulder in mute sympathy, and George shook his head as if forcibly dismissing painful memories.

"You use this desk." He pointed to the phone. "When a call comes in, answer it and then transfer it to the appropriate office. They're all clearly marked on the phone. If you aren't sure who it's for, route it to my secretary. What she doesn't know about the company isn't worth knowing.

"When people come in and want to see someone, check their names against the list of appointments scheduled for today." He pointed to a neatly typed sheet in the center of the desk. "If their name is there, have them go back to the appropriate office. Through there." He gestured toward a glass door in the opposite wall. "If their name isn't there, call who they want to see and let that person decide if they have time to squeeze them in."

Emily nodded. "It sounds clear enough."

"You shouldn't have any problems. It's not a very demanding job. Mostly you just need common sense and some tact. We use it as an entry-level position. As a matter of fact, we ran an ad for a new receptionist in the paper this morning. If anyone shows up to apply for it, send them to Personnel."

"Thank you for helping us out with our study." Emily gave him a warm smile, not noticing when he blinked under its impact.

"We'll see you later, George," Lucas said.

"Um, yes, for lunch. I hope you'll be my guests?"

"We'd love to," Lucas replied, accepting for both of them.

"You always were a lucky devil, Lucas," George whispered with a final glance at Emily who was putting her purse into one of the desk drawers. After giving her a final encouraging smile, he left.

"Lucky" didn't begin to describe it, Lucas thought. This time, he'd found the pot of gold at the end of the rainbow. Soon he'd be able to announce to the whole world that Emily belonged to him. The idea filled him with a primitive satisfaction that vaguely surprised him. Never before had he felt possessive about a woman, but he did with Emily. He wanted to post No Trespassing signs all around her. And he intended to begin the process with the largest diamond ring he could find—or, perhaps, a sapphire to match her eyes.

"Are you in there?" Emily's amused voice broke through his daydreams.

"Just planning." He smiled at her. "I think I'll sit here by the door. That'll give me a clear view of both you and anyone coming in."

Emily forced herself to concentrate on how the phone system worked, but her heart really wasn't in it. Her gaze kept straying back to Lucas. She ran the tip of her tongue over her bottom lip as she observed the breadth of his shoulders in the elegantly tailored gray suit he was wearing. Obligingly her mind supplied an image of those shoulders without the gray jacket. Likewise, a memory of the feel of his hot skin beneath her fingertips, of the ripple of his muscles as he moved over her, of—

Emily glanced down at the gleaming desktop to break the spell, telling herself that it was grossly inappropriate to sit ogling him like some love-struck adolescent. Someone might come in and catch her at it, and that could well influence how that person treated her.

Lucas's sound of disgust made her look up. "What's the matter?" she asked.

"*Your*. To say nothing of *too*."

"Well, if you want to be understood, you'd better say something else."

"It's grammar. Or, more specifically, the lack thereof in these papers." He gestured with the folder he was holding. "Some of these students don't seem to know the difference between *you're* with an apostrophe and without. And they appear to be totally in the dark as to when to spell *to* with two *o*s. They should have learned that in grade school," he added impatiently.

Emily shrugged. "And nations shouldn't fight wars and people shouldn't use drugs. The list of what shouldn't be is endless. All you can do is deal with what you have and not worry about what you should have."

"In a graduate-level business course?" he demanded in disbelief.

"Unfortunately, it's not just business students who have a problem with the written language. A lot of my history students have a very sketchy command of grammar. And what's worse, they don't seem to care."

"So, what do you do about it?" he asked. "How am I supposed to grade something like this?"

Emily sighed. "It depends on what you told them. When I give my first written assignment of the year, I tell my students exactly what I expect."

"And that is?"

"It depends on the level. In the freshman courses, I turn a blind eye to the atrocities they commit against the English language and base their grade on the historical content. Sophomore courses, I mark the grammar and spelling mistakes and give them a tentative grade based on the paper's contents. If they correct the mistakes and hand it in again, I give them the original grade. If they don't, I reduce the original grade by one letter. In their junior year, I simply mark two grades lower for excessive bad grammar and spelling."

"I see." Lucas thoughtfully rubbed his jaw. And Emily shifted uneasily in her seat as she remembered the raspy texture of that same jaw against her neck as he'd nuzzled her ear.

She swallowed and continued, "The important thing is to state your policy clearly and be consistent."

He grunted. "Does it count if I consistently feel infuriated?"

Emily laughed. "That, my friend, is an occupational hazard. A frequent—" The outer door opened.

Lucas hurriedly retreated behind his papers while Emily waited to see who'd arrived. It was a large, very overweight middle-aged man carrying a salesman's sample case. Emily gave him her best professional smile.

"Well, hello there, dollface," the man gushed. "You're new here, aren't you? Sure make the place look better. Where'd you come from?"

Emily gave him a limpid look. "My mother used to say that God sent me."

"If not from Him, then certainly from somewhere in heaven." He leered happily at her.

"Thank you." Emily found it impossible to be offended by his lechery; it was much too open. "May I help you?"

The man abruptly sobered. "You sure could, dollface. Tell me, what kind of mood is old George in this morning?"

"He seemed pretty much as usual," Emily ventured, hoping it was true.

"Damn!" The man grimaced. "I was kind of hoping that the sight of you would have made him more amenable."

"Might I point out that if what he wants is me, then the sight of you would make him less agreeable, not more," she retorted.

The man blinked and looked at her in surprise.

"If you'll just give me your name, Mr—?" She paused expectantly.

"Selming. Mike Selming." He frowned at her. "You know, you sure don't sound like any receptionist I ever ran across."

"I'm really overqualified for this job," Emily whispered as she checked to make sure he was indeed on the list of appointments, "but I couldn't find work in my own field."

"What is your field?"

"Neurosurgery." She gave him a bland smile. "If you want to go back to George's office now?"

"Neurosurgery!" he snorted, as he shifted his heavy case to his other hand and headed to the plant's offices.

"Dollface?" Lucas repeated incredulously once the man had disappeared from sight.

Emily giggled. "I kind of liked him."

"I liked him better when he left. Dollface!" he muttered and retreated behind his papers as the door opened again.

A young woman entered. Her makeup was too dark for her pale skin and not only was her dress ill-fitting, but it was much too strong a shade for her delicate blond coloring. Someone who would profit from the results of Marcy's study if ever she saw one, Emily thought.

Emily gave the young woman a warm, encouraging smile, but the reaction was not what she expected. The young woman gave her an agonized look and half turned as if to leave.

"May I help you, miss?" Emily's voice halted her.

"Well—" the woman picked nervously at the strap of her purse "—I wanted to fill out an application for the reception job that was advertised in the paper this morning, but if you're a sample of what they normally hire—"

She gestured helplessly.

"I'm temporary," Emily soothed. "Personnel is through there." Emily pointed to the glass door.

"Thank you," the woman murmured and scurried through the doors.

Lucas looked thoughtful as he watched the woman disappear. "Emily, you don't suppose someone else is doing the same research as Marcy, do you?"

"Not at this university. Marcy would know about it. Why?"

"Because that woman looks a little like you do when you're wearing your disguise. Although she couldn't touch you for looks if she were dressed up."

"Thanks, but I think her problem is simply lack of knowledge. She needs to read a few books. Ah-hah! Our next victim."

An immaculately dressed man about Lucas's age, carrying a sample case, approached her. Her professional smile slipped somewhat as the man stared at her in a manner she found distinctly offensive.

"May I help you?" Her voice was just this side of freezing.

"My name is Pelling and I have an appointment with Mr. Knight, so I'll just go on back."

"Pelling, you said?" Her voice effectively stopped him.

"Yes." The man frowned at her. "I have an appointment, and I don't want to be late."

"I'm sorry, but you aren't listed on the sheet. I'll call his secretary and ask if—"

"Then you must have forgotten to put me on it," he snapped, "because I know I made the appointment earlier in the week. Mr. Knight isn't going to like this."

"You mean if I were to let you interrupt him without an appointment?" Emily gave him an innocent smile. "I already know he wouldn't like it. That's why I'm being so careful."

"Let me give you my card with my name on it." Pelling pulled out his wallet and extracted a business card and a ten-dollar bill. He wrapped the bill around the card and handed both of them to her. "Does that help you find my appointment?" He smirked.

"On the contrary—" Emily handed the money back to him with a dismissive smile "—it convinces me that I was correct in the first place or you wouldn't be trying to bribe me now."

"Why you flashy little bitch! I'll—"

"You'll either accept her offer to ring Knight's secretary or you'll leave!" Lucas's hard voice broke into Pelling's tirade.

Pelling spread his fingers deprecatingly and gave Lucas an ingratiating smile. "Sorry, but she made a mistake that could cost me a sale and now she expects me to pay for it. You know what beautiful women are like." He gave Lucas a just-between-us-men look that made Emily long to smack him.

"I know what this one's like," Lucas responded cuttingly. "And, believe me, she doesn't make mistakes."

"Sorry," Pelling sneered. "I didn't realize I was trespassing on your preserve. I'll wait till the regular girl is back and deal with her." He stalked out.

"Phew!" Emily let her breath out on a long sigh. "And I thought teaching was stressful. This job ought to come with a whip and a chair. I wonder how he would have reacted to my disguise?"

"With any luck at all, we won't find out," Lucas snarled. "A jerk like that could give the whole male sex a bad name."

"I've got a news flash for you. Jerks like him already have. I shudder to think what else the day may bring."

But to Emily's relief, the rest of the day brought no one even vaguely approaching Pelling for sheer nastiness, even though it seemed to her exhausted mind that she greeted hundreds of people, all wanting something. By late afternoon, her face ached from the effort of maintaining a smiling countenance, and her muscles cramped protestingly from her unaccustomed inactivity.

Even a long, leisurely soak in a warm bath when she got home that evening only partially revived her. She was sprawled on her couch trying to work up the energy to do something constructive when her doorbell rang.

Emily felt a sudden surge of adrenaline at the thought it might be Lucas. Maybe his workshop had been canceled. She was vaguely appalled at the extent of the pleasure she felt at the idea of seeing him again. Especially considering the fact that they'd spent the greater part of the day together. No, not really together, she revised. They'd been in the same room, but as busy as she'd been, they'd had very little chance to do more than exchange glances, and George's reminiscences had dominated the conversation at lunch.

She hurried to the door and opened it to find Marcy standing there. Emily could almost feel her newfound energy draining out of her.

"I didn't expect a rapturous greeting, but a simple hello would have been nice," Marcy said.

Emily chuckled. "Sorry, I thought you were someone else. Come on in. I'd much rather talk to you than go over my least favorite graduate student's latest changes to his proposed dissertation."

"The one with the bent for torture?"

Emily sighed. "The one and only."

"What did you ever do about him?"

Emily flopped back down onto the sofa. "I decided to treat the committee as a group of rational human beings and not as a collection of male chauvinists. I told them exactly how I felt about what the student was researching."

"And?" Marcy prodded.

"And their reaction partially restored my faith in men. Only Dan Ellings gave me the squeamish-little-woman routine. And before he could really get started, Dave Morton interrupted him and said that as far as he was concerned, inflicting pain on other human beings was not a masculine trait. But then Ed Livengood admitted that he couldn't eat his dinner after he read the section on disembowelment."

"So, what is the committee going to do about it?"

Emily grimaced. "Nothing."

"Nothing! But—"

"We talked to Dr. Warren, who pointed out that we really don't have the right to censor academic research simply because we find the subject personally abhorrent."

Marcy frowned thoughtfully. "Much as I hate to admit it, the man does have a point."

"Yeah, we thought so, too. The committee finally decided that we did have the right to demand some objectivity in his dissertation. And speaking of objectives, Lucas and I spent the day working on your project."

"I remembered your plan for today. That's why I stopped by—to see how it had gone."

"Let me tell you, being a receptionist is a darn sight harder than I thought. I still don't believe that all those people who trailed through my area today could have had business at the plant." Emily heaved a gigantic sigh. "If that's a taste of the real world, I think I'll stick to my academic ivory tower, thank you."

"Forget the complaints. What did you discover?" Marcy leaned forward eagerly.

"You mean, besides the fact that I have unsympathetic friends?"

"Sympathy corrodes a person," replied Marcy, dismissing her ploy. "Quit stalling and tell me what you concluded."

"I concluded that I couldn't conclude anything."

"Emily!"

"No, I'm serious. I spent the morning gorgeous and the afternoon uglied up, and there was no really consistent reaction from the people coming into the office. I had a couple of people assume that since I was beautiful, I must be dumb, but they certainly weren't in the majority. Actually, I think that on average people were friendlier when I was uglier—especially the women."

Marcy wasn't surprised. "Makes sense. Physical perfection tends to be off-putting to a normal woman, and you are one of the most highly polished pieces of physical perfection I've ever seen."

Emily laughed. "I'll have to tell my parents that you approve of their genetic material."

"It's a real shame that they didn't have a few more kids," Marcy mourned. "I'd love to have seen what they looked like."

"Never mind genetics. I'm much more concerned with your study. If I were you, when you set up the real one, I'd try to keep your encounters as simple as possible. What we did today involved too many variables for us to be able to draw any conclusions."

"You could be right. Most of the other things you've done have been one-on-one. Are you and Lucas still planning on finishing up tomorrow night?"

"Uh-huh. All we have left is me sitting alone in a bar. I can type up our notes over the weekend and drop them off at your office Monday morning."

"Great! That'll give me plenty of time to analyze your data before I set up the real study."

"I've got news for you, Marcy. It doesn't get any 'realer' than today," Emily said ruefully.

"Speaking of Lucas," Marcy interjected.

"I didn't realize we were."

Marcy eyed her closely as if trying to decide what to say. "Do you mind if I ask you something personal?"

"Not if you don't mind if I don't answer."

"You like Lucas, don't you?"

"What's not to like?"

"Emily!" Marcy wailed in frustration.

"Marcy, I'm long past the age of exchanging girlish confidences on a man's prowess as a lover."

"Ah-hah!" Marcy looked triumphant. "I knew it. I took one look at the guy and knew he'd be perfect for you."

"In an earlier age, you'd have been burned at the stake for witchcraft."

"I just knew it," Marcy chortled, ignoring Emily's crack. "Tell me, what did he say about your operation? Emily?" Marcy stopped at the expression on her friend's face. "You haven't told him?"

"I tried," Emily defended herself. "I really tried, but I just couldn't find the words. And, anyway, it doesn't make any difference. Lucas has never said anything that would lead me to believe that he has permanency in mind, let alone children." She had no intention of mentioning Lucas's abusive childhood, even to Marcy.

"Emily, you've got to tell him," Marcy insisted. "The man has a right to know."

"What about my right to privacy?" Emily shot back.

"It seems to me that you already gave up that right where he's concerned."

Emily sighed. "Yeah, in a big way. Marcy, I really...care about Lucas. If he bolts because I can't have children..."

For the first time, Marcy questioned the wisdom of what she'd done. What if she'd been wrong? What if Lucas did cut and run? His defection might drive Emily so far back into her shell she'd never emerge.

"He won't care," Marcy insisted, trying desperately to believe it herself. "The man's thirty-six years old. As you say, if he had wanted kids, surely he'd have done something about it before now."

A tantalizing memory of Lucas helping that small boy out of the apple tree surfaced, but Emily refused to dwell on it. Marcy had to be right, because if she wasn't, the alternative was too devastating to even consider.

"Just make sure you tell him tomorrow night," Marcy ordered. "But for now, why don't we get a pizza, rent a few movies and make a night of it?"

"You're on." Emily eagerly consigned the problem to the future.

UNFORTUNATELY, "the future" arrived the following evening when Lucas came to escort her to the bar and Emily still had no clear-cut idea how to break the news. She couldn't just blurt it out. She needed to find a way to gradually lead into it.

Emily studied him anxiously as she tried to figure out how to broach the topic.

"Why so serious?" Lucas smoothed away a worry line between her arched brows. "I'll be there to protect you."

Emily tried to ignore the instant flare of desire that shot through her at his casual touch. This was awful! She was becoming so attuned to him that the slightest physical contact with him was enough to drive all other thoughts from her mind.

"You know, Emily, we don't have to go through with this," he said seriously. "In fact, if you'll remember correctly, I was against the idea of the bar from the beginning. And I'm even more against it when I see how you look tonight." His gaze roamed over her slim body, lighting fires where it touched.

Emily licked her dry lips. "What's wrong with the way I look?"

"You look like the embodiment of every fantasy I and ninety percent of the world's male population ever had. That's what's wrong. And that dress—what there is of it—" he gestured toward the plunging neckline "—clings to your body like a second skin. And not only that, but that color—"

Emily blinked in surprise. "I like fuchsia."

"It's too forthcoming for a bar," he countered stubbornly.

Emily swallowed a grin at his aggrieved expression, secretly pleased at his show of possessiveness even though she had absolutely no intention of giving in to it.

"Well," she replied slowly, as if giving the matter careful consideration, "I have a black outfit I could wear. It has a very full skirt and a shirtwaist top."

"That's the ticket." He nodded happily.

"Of course, the blouse is transparent silk organza."

"Transparent?" He looked at her in shock.

"Uh-huh. It has strategically placed gold leaves painted on it."

"They can't be that strategically placed," he remarked dryly. "What I want to know is where on earth you wore it around here?"

"I haven't," she admitted sheepishly. "I bought it on a trip to New York City, but I've never had the nerve to actually wear it anywhere."

"Tell you what." His eyes began to glow with a warmth that found an answering flare of heat deep inside her. "You can model it for me one evening."

But would he still want her to, once he knew about her sterility? That possibility extinguished her desire. "Lucas," she began impulsively and then just as impulsively stopped. She postponed the inevitable: She'd tell him when they got back. If she told him now, it might upset the rest of the study, she rationalized.

Lucas frowned at her. "What's wrong, Emily? You've been tense enough to break ever since I came through the door."

"Nothing." She grabbed her evening purse from the hall table and yanked open the door, giving him no option but to follow her out.

"Where exactly are we going?" he asked when they were in his car.

"The bar down at the Wyatt Hotel. We should be able to attract a good cross section of men there."

Later, it seemed to Lucas's jaundiced view that they had got far too many men in her cross section. From the moment Emily had perched on a stool at the other end of the bar from him, there had been a continuous stream of men trying to pick her up. He took an impatient gulp of his mineral water and glanced at his watch. Another half hour and he'd take her back to put on her disguise. Then, perhaps, he'd get some peace. This had to have been the most frustrating evening of his life. He wanted to publicly stand up and claim Emily as his; instead, he was forced to sit and watch while every would-be Lothario within a hundred-mile radius tried his luck at talking her into bed.

And it wasn't just that, he thought sourly. It was Emily herself. She kept darting him nervous little glances as if she expected him to turn into a jealous-crazed man at any minute. What could have happened to have suddenly resurrected all her old doubts about him?

Perhaps he was playing too cautious a hand. Maybe he should tell her now what he planned for their future. Maybe that was all she needed—the security of actually hearing him say that he wanted to spend the rest of his life with her. But then, who was he kidding? He didn't want her; he needed her. *Craved* her. She was as necessary to his well-being as food and water. *So, tell her!* he ordered himself. *Tell her tonight and put both of you out of your misery.*

He glanced at Emily again, and his features hardened into angry lines as the cretin she'd been talking to suddenly laid his hand on her bare knee.

"That's it!" He didn't care if the fate of the whole free world hung on Marcy's damned study; no man was mauling his woman.

"Hey, good-looking, how's about you and I go make beautiful music together?" The man's hand inched under her skirt.

"If you don't remove your hand, the only music you're likely to hear is a host of heavenly angels," Lucas bit out from behind them.

"Now, just a minute, buddy." The man turned around, moving with the exaggerated care of the almost-drunk, and his face paled. Not even the alcohol he'd consumed was enough to blind him to the fury darkening Lucas's face.

"I think you'd better go," Emily murmured to the man and turned, with a placating glance, to the bartender who'd been giving her suspicious looks all evening. "This is my boyfriend, and his parole officer doesn't like it when he gets into fights in bars."

"Parole—" The man's eyes bulged and he edged off his seat, being careful to keep it between him and Lucas. "Sorry, buddy. I didn't know she was taken," he muttered and scurried out.

"Come on." Lucas grabbed her arm and hauled her to her feet.

"You all right, miss?" The bartender eyed Lucas with some of the same nervousness the drunk had shown.

Emily gave the man a warm smile. Poor soul. He'd probably spent the evening wondering what was going on. "I'm Dr. McGregor from the university and this is Lucas Sheridan, who's helping me with a study."

"So that's it!" The man grinned. "I wondered what you were up to. I mean, you kept attracting everything in pants, but you didn't keep them, so to speak. I thought you were a high-priced call girl and none of them could afford you."

"And on that note, we'll leave." Lucas firmly pulled her away from the bar.

"A call girl!" Emily sputtered. "Did you ever hear the like?"

"No. But if you continue to help Marcy with her projects, I'm sure you'll eventually hear worse," he said in resignation.

"That is the last bit of research I do for her, no matter what she says!" Emily raged. "If she wants an 'ugly' version of tonight, she can do it herself. Call girl, indeed!"

"High-priced call girl." Lucas chuckled. "I think he meant it as a compliment."

"Compliment!" Emily stalked out of the hotel's front door. "I'd like to compliment him!"

"Forget him. I'm hungry. How about if we get some carryout from that Chinese place over by the mall and go back to your apartment? You could model your strategically placed gold leaves for me."

Emily saw the gleam in his eyes and her outrage was suddenly replaced by another, much more potent emotion.

"You're on."

12

"THE MASTER BEDROOM should have a television set in it," Lucas suddenly announced.

"Hmm?" Emily snuggled closer to his hard, muscled body.

"I'm serious. We're missing the Saturday-morning cartoons." Lucas's hand absently rubbed over her bare back. "It would be better with a television."

Emily laughed. "It doesn't get any better than this. Besides, this isn't a master bedroom. This is my room. Therefore it's the mistress's bedroom, and mistresses don't have televisions in their rooms."

"Mistresses have no imagination. We'll put one in the master suite of the house."

"What house?" Emily stopped winding the hair on his chest around her finger and peered up into his face.

"The one I intend to build. Remember? I told you that if I liked teaching I'd accept a permanent appointment and build a house. I was talking to the dean of the School of Architecture last week and he recommended someone to design it for me. Once we decide on a property, we can call the man."

Emily felt an incandescent bubble of joy at his use of the word *we*. It sounded very much as if Lucas was planning on including her in his future.

"I saw a property yesterday that had about five acres to it."

"That's a lot of grass to mow," Emily remarked, trying to figure out how to get him to be more specific about exactly how she fitted into his long-range plans without coming right out and asking.

"I thought we could have a big garden and a small orchard and a stable with enough pasture for a couple of horses."

Emily laughed. "Horses? Are you planning on producing your own organic fertilizer?"

"I always wanted a horse when I was young," he admitted.

"Every kid wants a horse."

"So it's reasonable to assume that ours will. What do you say to two?"

Emily swallowed on the metallic taste of pain at the shock of his unexpected words, numbing her thought processes and slowing her heartbeat to a dull, erratic thudding that echoed hollowly in her ears.

"Two horses?" she whispered, trying to absorb the shock without giving herself away.

"No, kids. I always felt sorry for only children because when anything happened, their parents always knew who to blame.

"You do like kids, don't you?" Lucas asked uncertainly, beginning to pick up on her tension.

"Oh, yes." Her sincerity was unmistakable.

Lucas frowned as Emily climbed off the bed and slipped on her housecoat, with jerky, uncoordinated movements. "I always planned to have a family," he continued. "I'm just a couple of years ahead of schedule, thanks to you."

"Oh?" Emily bit the inside of her lower lip to stop its trembling. She felt as if she were coming apart inside. As if all her hopes and dreams for their future together had just shattered into a thousand fragments and the sharp pieces were slicing through her flesh. All she could think about was that she couldn't let Lucas know the mortal blow his casual words had dealt her. She couldn't bear to have his feelings for her turn to pity. Anything was better than pity.

She drew a long, shaky breath, praying for the strength to send him away. Then she could break down. Not before.

Lucas got out of bed and began to dress, surreptitiously watching Emily as he did so. What was wrong? They'd been in absolute accord just a few minutes ago. So what had sent her a million miles away from him? He automatically tied his shoes, his attention still focused on her rigidly held body that seemed to put him at such a distance.

Surely his reference to their future couldn't have done it. He'd seen the glow in her eyes when he'd first mentioned the house. Could it be the permanency of marriage that she objected to? He frowned. That didn't make any sense. Emily was a very committed kind of person. And she loved him. He was as sure of that as he was of his own feelings for her. They might never have actually spoken the words aloud, but they hadn't really needed to. Her feelings were clearly expressed every time he took her in his arms. So, what the hell was the matter?

"I think you'd better go." Emily's voice was thin, unlike her, and it sent a chill of foreboding through him.

"But we need to decide when you can see the property the real-estate agent showed me." He stalled for time.

"I'm not going to." She forced the words out past lips that seemed frozen. "Your plans for the future have nothing to do with me."

"Don't be ridiculous, Emily," he said roughly. "We're going to be married just as soon as it can be arranged."

"No," Emily retorted harshly. "We aren't. Please go."

"Please go!" he echoed incredulously. "That's it? Please go! It's been nice tumbling around in bed with you and now would you please go? Hell no, lady! I won't 'please go.' I want to know what's going on."

"I don't owe you any explanations," she answered tightly. "Just as you don't owe me anything."

"To hell with what I owe you! I want to *give* you everything!"

Emily closed her eyes as his words beat into her. If only she could give him what he wanted—children. But she couldn't. Not now. Not ever. And she couldn't tell him, because Lucas was essentially a very kind man. He'd never take back his proposal. He'd tell her it didn't matter, and he'd try hard to believe it. But in the end, his desire for children would erode his feelings for her until all that would be left would be pity and bitterness and regret.

"Please go," she repeated doggedly.

"Emily." He reached for her, wincing as she jerked away.

He tried to force his mind past the fear that was filling him. Maybe he needed to give her time. "All right," he finally said. "I've obviously taken you by surprise. I'll call you this evening and we can talk then."

Emily watched him leave, holding herself stiffly against the agony filling her. When she heard her front door slam behind him, the iron will she'd been exerting dissolved. She sagged against the wall and slowly slipped to the floor. She was too full of pain to even cry. Nothing in her life had ever hurt this much. She didn't see how she could bear it, but she'd have to. She'd have to smile and act normally or Lucas would find out. All she had left was her pride. She couldn't surrender that, too.

BY EVENING, Emily had managed to achieve a measure of calm. That it was shock induced didn't worry her. She was simply grateful for the numbness. When she picked up the ringing phone at ten and found it was Lucas, she was able to cut through his carefully casual greeting and tell him that she didn't want to talk to him and hang up. Even the sight of her trembling fingers still clutching the receiver barely registered. It was as if her individual body parts were detached from her mind.

Lucas, unfortunately, felt none of her blessed numbness as he stared at the dead receiver he was gripping. He was filled with a mixture of rage, frustration and futility; and underlying it all was a growing sense of fear. He needed answers, and he didn't even know what the questions were.

Lucas hung up the phone and stared at the wall as he tried to think. *Marcy,* he suddenly remembered. Marcy was Emily's friend from their graduate-school days. If anyone knew what was eating away at Emily, Marcy would.

He grabbed his car keys and rushed out. He had to talk to her now, but he had no intention of calling first and warning her he was coming. If he gave her time to think things over, Marcy might decide that loyalty to Emily dictated that she not tell him anything.

Marcy answered her door on his second knock. The perfectly natural smile she gave him convinced him that she hadn't talked to Emily yet.

"Hi, Lucas," she said. "Come on in. Is Emily with you?"

"No." He walked into her living room and began to pace, trying to decide where to begin. He quickly gave up and came right to the point: "Why would Emily come unglued when I mentioned marriage?"

"Unglued?" Marcy echoed apprehensively.

"Unglued as in 'gone away in her mind.'" He gestured impatiently. "It doesn't matter what you call it. The result is that she shut me out completely. One minute we were discussing buying a lot with enough space for the kids to have horses, and—"

Marcy stared at him in dread.

"What the hell is it about the mention of horses that produces that kind of reaction in women?" he demanded.

"Um, well . . ." Marcy closed her eyes in negation of the whole mess. Why, oh why, hadn't she minded her own business and left Emily to work out her problem in her own time?

"Maybe it's me." Lucas threw up his hands in frustration. "Maybe there's something about me that sends educated women into trances."

"It's not you." The strongly developed nurturing part of Marcy's personality automatically responded.

"Then it *is* something?" Lucas pounced on her choice of words. "What?"

"Ask Emily."

"I did," he gritted out. "And got exactly nowhere."

"If Emily wants you to know, she'll tell you," Marcy finally said. "I've already interfered enough. I think you'd better leave."

"Damn!" Lucas stormed out of her apartment, deriving a temporary satisfaction from slamming her front door behind him. He climbed into his Porsche and pulled out into the deserted street with a shriek of burning rubber.

"Ask Emily!" he snorted. *How the hell am I supposed to ask Emily anything when she won't even talk to me?*

By refusing to leave until she explained what had turned her from a loving woman into a cold, remote stranger. He turned around and headed back toward Emily's apartment building.

Her car was still in its parking space, and he breathed a sigh of relief. He'd been half afraid she might run away, and he didn't want to wait until he'd tracked her down. He wanted this settled now.

He sprinted up the stairs and paused in front of her doorway. Taking a deep breath, he pushed the bell. After what seemed like an age to his worn nerves, he heard her footsteps approaching. To his disappointment, she didn't open the door; she called through it. "Who's there?"

"The Fuller Brush man," he snapped. "Open the door, Emily. I want to talk to you."

"There's nothing to talk about." The deadness in her voice frightened him. How could he have hurt her so badly and not even know what he'd done?

"Emily, love—" he tried for a softer tone that didn't quite come off "—you can't hide forever. I'm not going to gracefully ride off into the sunset unless you agree to come with me. We have to talk this out."

"No," she said wearily.

He bit back a very real urge to kick in the door. "Emily, either you open the door and talk to me or I'll sit here until you do."

"Go away." Her voice cracked, and he felt a shaft of frustrated pain at the sound.

"I'm going to wait," he warned stubbornly. "You can't stay holed up in there forever."

Emily listened to the sounds he made as he sat down in the hallway and leaned back against her door. Slowly, she knelt in front of it and placed her palms flat against the wood. She could almost feel his warmth through the door. Her breath caught in her throat as she realized what she was doing, and she rocked back on her heels. Lucas was stubborn enough to sit there all night. And he was right. She couldn't stay holed up in here for any length of time, even if she wanted to. She had classes to teach on Monday morning.

She got to her feet and rubbed her aching head, trying to decide how to handle the situation, when she heard the unmistakable sound of Everard's growls.

Emily tensed as she heard Mrs. Kitchener's footsteps a second later.

"Why it's Emily's friend, that nice Mr. Sheridan," her neighbor said. "No, dear," she admonished the dog. "We mustn't snap at him. Isn't Emily back yet, Mr. Sheridan? If you like, you may wait at my apartment for her. I'm sure she'll be along soon. She is usually— No, Everard!"

Emily winced at the sound of Everard's growl.

"Thank you, Mrs. Kitchener, but Emily's inside." Lucas raised his voice slightly. "She just won't let me in."

"Won't let you in?" Mrs. Kitchener repeated in confusion.

"Yes. She led me on and trifled with my affections, and now she refuses to marry me." He lowered his voice conspiratorially. "She told me to go away."

Emily leaned her head against the door, not knowing whether to laugh or cry.

"Surely not!" Mrs. Kitchener sounded scandalized. "And she always seemed like a nice girl, too. That just goes to show that you never can tell about people, doesn't it?"

Emily pressed her eyelids shut and took a deep breath. She was going to have to tell Lucas. Clumsily, she opened the door.

"It's about time," he said, pushing past her.

Emily closed the door on Mrs. Kitchener's disapproving face and hesitantly followed him into the living room. Lucas strode over to the window and looked out. Now that he was inside, he seemed no more eager for a confrontation than she had been.

She watched as the late-evening light pouring through the window gilded his dark hair. Hungrily she drank in the sight, storing up the memory against the loneliness of her future.

He finally turned. "Emily—"

"No." She cut him off. Now she couldn't bear to delay this confrontation. "You demanded an explanation. I'll give it to you. It's very simple, really. I can't have children." Her tone was flat from the effort it took to keep from crying.

Lucas stared at her in shock as her words echoed eerily through his mind, seeming to gain volume with each repetition. "You mean you don't want children?" He enunciated each word carefully, as if his very precision could make them true.

"I mean I am physically incapable of having them," she replied harshly as her control wavered slightly. "I had fibroid tumors, and the doctor had to take my uterus out last spring."

Lucas shook his head in instinctive denial of her words. Emily couldn't be sterile! They were going to have children and be a real family like the one he'd always wanted to belong to. This had to be some kind of mistake!

Emily watched the shocked disbelief in his eyes as he struggled to come to terms with her words. As one would struggle to come to terms with death. She glanced down, unable to bear the sight of his beloved features set in such harsh lines. She was responsible for the pain he was feeling.

Her eyes fell to her hand, which was clenched so tightly that the knuckles were bone white. She tried to relax, but her fingers seemed to have a mind of their own. It was as if they were afraid to let go for fear that she would be swept away into oblivion by the weight of her despair.

"Emily." Lucas forced her name out past lips that felt numb. He watched as she flinched. Emily was hurting. *She needed him.* That single thought surfaced through the maelstrom of emotion that was buffeting him. Emily needed him, and he had to do something. He took a tentative step toward her.

"No!" She instinctively held out a hand to ward him off. *Not pity. Dear God, not pity! Not from Lucas.* She'd seen his reaction to her words. There was no way she could continue to delude herself that he wouldn't care that she was sterile. A blind man could have seen that he most assuredly did. It mattered desperately to him.

If she'd just been honest from the beginning... A tremor shook her, radiating outward, and Emily locked her muscles in an attempt to control her trembling. She had to end this confrontation, she thought agitatedly. She just couldn't take any more pain. Not her own, not his. She felt as if she were drowning in it, and the truly frightening thing was that she wasn't even sure she wanted to fight it. At this moment, oblivion seemed a blessing.

"Lucas, if you feel anything at all for me, leave me my pride." She stared at him through a film of tears—tears that she fought a desperate battle to keep from falling. "Please believe that I never meant this to happen. I know I should have told you sooner, but, at first, I didn't think you wanted anything more than an affair.

And, when I began to suspect that you might have permanency in mind, I found out about your miserable childhood and I thought you wouldn't want children." Her lips lifted in a travesty of a smile. "Or maybe I was simply rationalizing. I don't know, and at this point it no longer matters. Just go and leave me in peace. Please!" Her voice cracked.

"Emily," he began urgently.

"Don't you see? There's nothing you can say. Your expression when I told you has already said it all." She gulped, swallowing air and tears and the bitter taste of defeat. "For God's sake, just go!"

Lucas shoved his fists into his pants pockets and left. He didn't know what else to do. He felt murderous. He wanted to smash something, to rant and rave and curse at fate. But he knew Emily couldn't cope with his emotions.

Instinct carried him to his car and he got in and drove, winding up at the property the real-estate agent had shown him. He cut the Porsche's engine and leaned over the steering wheel, studying the land with a feeling of bitter irony.

Yesterday, when he'd seen the huge maple tree, he'd envisioned an old-fashioned swing with Emily pushing a shrieking toddler. The spreading oak in the back had seemed the perfect site for a tree house for a pair of youthful pirates. He'd almost been able to see Emily sending up snacks to the children by way of a lowered bucket. His gaze traveled on to the very back of the property where he'd planned to put in their orchard so that Emily could pass on the tradition of making applesauce to their daughter.

But Emily was never going to have his daughter. His carefully formulated life plan had suddenly been derailed.

He snorted in self-derision. He'd been so smugly sure of himself and his ability to get what he wanted. First, a college degree, then so many years to make all the money he'd ever need, then a change to a less time-consuming career, and finally, once his second career was established, a wife and a family.

And it had all gone according to plan. Right up to the time for his family. So now what? He forced himself to view this as a business problem. Essentially, he had two choices: He could marry Emily and forego children, or he could marry someone else and have children.

He surveyed the empty acres again and frowned as he realized that every time he'd pictured his children doing something, Emily had been beside them. Never had he fantasized about the children alone. Always, there had been Emily.

The two of them fitted together so perfectly. He simply couldn't imagine a life without her. In fact, the wonder was that he'd managed to survive the thirty-six years before he'd met her.

He sighed, feeling as if a tremendous load had just been lifted from his shoulders. When it came right down to it, the only nonnegotiable thing in his life was Emily. All he had to do was to convince her of that fact.

He started the Porsche and headed back to town.

EMILY SPLASHED ICY WATER on her red, swollen eyes, but it didn't help much. She still looked awful. And she felt even worse. She swallowed against an urge to burst into tears again. She had to stop crying. All it did was give her a headache and a sore throat.

Listlessly, she trailed back into the living room. She jumped when the phone rang and stared at it, but made no attempt to pick it up. She wandered out into the kitchen and took a sofa out of the refrigerator. She pressed the icy metal can against her aching forehead and sighed with relief when the tight band encircling her head eased fractionally.

The phone finally stopped ringing, and she went back into the living room. To her dismay, the doorbell rang. The sound grated painfully on her already raw nerves. She stared blankly at the door. She had no intention of opening it. She couldn't face anyone at the moment, let alone deal with them. The way she felt, she didn't think she could ever face anyone again. This was worse—much worse—than when she'd discovered that she wouldn't be able to have children. Then, all she'd lost was the *possibility* of children. This time, she knew exactly who and what she'd lost.

As if her mind had conjured him out of the depths of her own longing, Emily heard his beloved voice.

"Open the damn door, Emily, or I swear I'll pick the lock!"

An involuntary smile lifted her lips. He probably would, too, she thought in resignation.

"Emily!"

Slowly she got to her feet, knowing that she was going to have to talk to him. To listen to him explain how sorry he was and how he hoped they'd always be friends.

She blinked back tears. It didn't matter how much it hurt. She had to try and make it easy for him. She loved him too much not to. She opened the door, lifting her gaze no higher than the second button of his yellow shirt. She couldn't bear to look into his eyes and see pity.

He stepped inside and kicked the door shut behind him. He cupped her chin and raised her head so that he could see her blotched, swollen face.

"You look like hell," he muttered a second before his arms closed around her with bruising force. He held her so tightly she could feel the thudding of his heartbeat echoing in her ears.

For a brief second she allowed herself the luxury of leaning against him, of drawing strength from him. Finally, her sense of self-preservation asserted itself and she tried to step back. His arms tightened.

"Lucas—" She winced at the raw, raspy sound of her voice. "Lucas," she repeated, "we have to talk."

"Yes." He let her go with a reluctance that lit a tiny flame of hope in her chilled heart.

She sat down on the edge of the sofa and twisted her fingers together. A great surge of tenderness shook him when he saw her obvious agitation. He wanted to take her back into his arms and kiss all her worries away, but he knew she was right. They had to talk, to settle her doubts once and for all.

Emily took a deep breath, uncertain where to begin. His greeting had unnerved her and thrown her off balance. "I realize that my sterility has come as a shock to you and that it changes everything, but—"

"No," he said flatly. "Some things, yes. But it doesn't change how I feel about you. It doesn't change the fact that I want to marry you and spend the rest of my life with you."

Emily closed her eyes to shut out his dear face and forced herself to think when every fiber of her being was urging her to fling herself back into his arms and accept his words at face value. But she couldn't. This was too important. For both their sakes, she had to make sure that Lucas really understood what he was giving up; that his words weren't simply a compassionate impulse.

"Lucas," she said slowly, "you aren't thinking clearly."

Unexpectedly, he laughed. "So, what else is new? I never have thought any too clearly around you. My feelings keep getting in the way."

"Well, feel what not having any children would be like," she told him, forcing the words out. "Feel what it would be like not to be able to regale your friends with your offsprings' latest accomplishments. Feel what it would be like never to have a child run up to you when you get home from work and fling his arms around you simply because he thinks you're the most wonderful father in the world. Feel what it would be like never to experience the wide-eyed wonder of your child on Christmas morning. Never to have grandchildren to spoil. Never—" Her voice finally broke as she listed the images that had haunted her ever since her operation. "Lucas, think, dammit! You'd never have a family!"

"I'd have you," he countered simply. "You and I would be a family. Emily, a family starts with a man and a woman sharing their love. And in the end, after all the kids are grown and gone, all that's left are a man and a woman still sharing that love. I don't deny that the bonds of blood are compelling, but the bonds of the heart are the strongest ties in the world."

"But you'd never have any children!" she shouted at him in frustration at his seeming inability to understand what she was saying.

Lucas frowned at her. "Are you unalterably opposed to adoption?"

"No, of course not." She gestured impotently. "But wouldn't you feel cheated not having your own children? After all, there's nothing wrong with *you*."

"Tell me, Emily, if our positions were reversed and I was the one who was sterile, would you go looking for another man?"

"Of course not!" she replied in shock. "How could you even think I would?"

"Then why are you crediting me with less ability to love than you have?"

Emily rubbed her brow in confusion. Her head hurt so badly that she found it difficult to think clearly. "It's just that—"

"Emily, listen to me." He crouched in front of her and took her icy fingers in his. "I went out and thought. I thought about you and me and the children I'd someday hoped to have. What I quickly realized was that I can cut out those nebulous dreams, but if I cut you out, I'd be cutting out my own heart. What I'm trying to say is that nothing matters in the end but you. Not my money, not my teaching, not my might-have-been children. Please, Emily, don't throw away what we do have simply because it doesn't contain everything you wanted."

Emily searched his eyes, almost afraid to believe what she was hearing. His eyes were full of love. They glowed with an unmistakable light. She felt an answering burst of joy so great she felt light-headed with it. It wasn't what society expected of her that mattered, she suddenly realized. It was what Lucas expected of her. And Lucas loved her. Loved her for what she was and not for what she could give him.

"Yes, oh, yes, my darling!" Joyously, she flung herself into his arms and as they closed around her, she felt whole as she never had in her life.

Epilogue

"LUCAS!" Emily burst into the kitchen, letting the door bang shut behind her. She started to step over the large mound of brown fur lying in the middle of the cream ceramic floor and then paused momentarily to study it.

Lucas looked up from the cake he was decorating and over to the sleeping dog. "What's the matter?"

She shook her head. "Nothing. I just wanted to make sure he was still breathing. He is the most placid animal I've ever seen and when I remember what he was like as a puppy..." She grinned as she suddenly remembered what she'd come in to show Lucas.

"Lucas, I finally found a use for beer." She gestured with the shallow metal pie plate she was carrying.

"I suppose it's too much to hope that you've started drinking it?"

"Do I look like I've taken leave of my senses?" She leaned against the center island where he was working and filched a taste of the icing.

Lucas's bright gaze swept over her oversize yellow sweatshirt to linger on the curves of her long legs, faithfully outlined by her worn jeans. "Actually—" his voice dropped to a husky whisper "—you look good enough to eat." He leaned toward her, frowning when he got a good look at the pie plate she'd set on the counter.

He sniffed the yellowish liquid in it and then demanded, "Why did you put my beer in that pie plate and what are those disgusting-looking gray blobs on the bottom?"

"Slugs!"

"Slugs?" he repeated questioningly.

"Uh-huh. I got the idea from a gardening book. It said that slugs like the taste of beer and when they crawl into a dish to get some, they drown."

"Good Lord." Lucas shook his head. "I should never have tilled that first garden patch for you. I've created a monster."

"An insatiable monster." Emily gave him her best come-hither look. "Just as soon as you've—" She frowned as their front doorbell rang. She glanced back at the dog. Typically, he hadn't stirred. "I wonder who could be calling at nine o'clock on a Saturday morning?"

"You could answer it and find out," Lucas suggested as he sprinkled chocolate shavings on the top of the cake.

"You answer it," Emily said firmly. "You're much better at getting rid of door-to-door salesmen than I am."

"It's a talent." He dropped a quick kiss on her parted lips, and Emily shivered. Two years of marriage had only strengthened the desire she felt for him.

"Although—" Lucas followed her out of the kitchen and toward the front of the house "—lack of sales resistance isn't all bad. We're the only people I know who still have Girl Scout cookies in the freezer five months after the sale."

"That poor little Brownie couldn't have been more than six and she needed to sell seventy-one more boxes to get her free T-shirt," Emily explained.

She peered out the long, narrow window that framed the door, paling when she saw who was there.

"Emily, what's the matter?" Lucas asked in concern.

"It's our caseworker from the adoption agency," Emily whispered. "What's she doing here? Last month she said it'd be at least another two years before we came to the top of the list of adoptive parents."

Lucas gave her a comforting squeeze. "She was probably just in the neighborhood and decided to stop in."

"Sure, and pigs may fly," Emily muttered. "That lady doesn't do anything without a good reason."

"Quit worrying." Lucas reached around her and opened the door.

"Good morning, Betty." Emily gave the woman what she hoped was a warm smile. "Won't you come in?"

"Thank you." Betty followed Emily into the huge formal living room to their right. "It's hard to believe that it's only the middle of May, the weather is so lovely."

"Yes, isn't it." Emily followed Betty's lead, almost choking when she looked up and caught the gleam of laughter in Lucas's eyes at the banality of the conversation.

Betty settled her ample figure on the long cream sofa and waited while Emily took a seat in one of the over-stuffed chintz-covered chairs across from her. Emily breathed an inward sigh of relief when Lucas sat on the arm of her chair. The feel of his warm thigh pressed up against her arm gave her a sense of security.

"You must be wondering what I'm doing here." Betty came to the point with a suddenness that instantly put Emily on her guard.

"Something happened three days ago that made me think of you and Lucas. Or, more precisely, made me think of the teeth marks on your piano leg."

Emily winced as she surreptitiously glanced at the baby-grand piano behind them. "Drat, I thought I'd covered them up with black crayon."

"I'm very observant when it comes to potential homes for one of the agency's babies," Betty continued. "And when I realized that you still had the dog who made them . . ."

"Silas had a few problems when he was a pup," Emily defended him, "but he soon outgrew them."

"In fact," Lucas added, "he seems to have outgrown movement of any kind. But I must admit to being a little confused. What does our dog's teething problems have to do with anything?"

"It's not the marks. It's your attitude toward them. It was how you took them in stride," Betty explained. "That was what convinced me that you'd be the ideal candidates for an unusual adoption that has come up."

Emily tensed at Betty's words, barely noticing when Lucas's hand closed over her shoulder.

"Are you telling us that you have a baby for us?" Lucas questioned.

"Possibly. Now, hear me out before you say anything," she warned when Emily literally bounced in her chair. "I want it clearly understood that if you decide against this adoption, it will not prejudice your place on our list. You'll continue to work your way to the top and you'll probably get a baby two years from this coming fall."

"Go on," Lucas urged, when Betty paused as if gathering her thoughts.

"The agency presently has an adoption available that is going to require a set of parents with patience, time and a very laid-back attitude toward their possessions. And, to be frank, it's also going to require a much larger financial output over the years than would normally be the case."

"What's wrong? Can it be corrected surgically, and when can we have the baby?" Emily fired the questions at Betty.

"It's not *a* baby," Betty said. "It's *three* babies. Triplets. And other than being smaller than the pediatrician would like, they're in perfect health. The mother had excellent prenatal care."

"Triplets?" Emily's incredulous response was drowned out by Lucas's shout of happiness.

"Identical boys and a girl." Betty smiled indulgently at Emily's expression.

"Thank goodness we went with our original plans and built the house with four bedrooms," Emily interjected.

"When can we bring our children home?" Lucas demanded.

"You can sign the adoption papers first thing Monday morning, and you can bring them home just as soon as they each reach five pounds. The pediatrician says the little girl should weigh that in a week or so, the boys slightly later. That'll give you a chance to get your nursery furniture in place.

"There's one more thing..." Betty continued slowly. "During our initial conversation when you first applied to adopt, you said that you were willing to allow the birth mother to remain in contact with the child."

"Yes." Emily nodded. "We feel that while it might cause problems on occasion, it will be better for our child—children," she corrected, "to know their background from the start."

Betty sighed in relief. "Good. The babies' mother doesn't feel able to raise them, but she does want to keep in touch. She graduated from a small private college in the northern part of the state last January and she's been accepted for the fall semester at medical school in New York City. So in the early years the contact will be mostly by letter."

"We could easily take them to see her a couple of times a year, once they're past the infant stage," Lucas offered.

"Excellent." Betty nodded decisively. "I knew the minute I saw that piano leg that you'd work out. Now, then, if you want to come with me I'll drive you over to the hospital and introduce you to your children."

"Yes!" Lucas and Emily exchanged a look of such unadulterated love that Betty's eyes misted over. "Let's go meet the lucky kids who are going to have Emily for a mother."

CHRISTMAS

STORIES · 1991

Bring back heartwarming memories of Christmas past
with HISTORICAL CHRISTMAS STORIES 1991,
a collection of romantic stories
by three popular authors.
The perfect Christmas gift!

Don't miss these heartwarming stories,
available in November
wherever Harlequin books are sold:

CHRISTMAS YET TO COME
by Lynda Trent
A SEASON OF JOY
by Caryn Cameron
FORTUNE'S GIFT
by DeLoras Scott

**Best Wishes and Season's Greetings
from Harlequin!**